59

# jink

AN INNER SANCTUM MYSTERY

## THOMAS PATRICK McMAHON

Simon and Schuster

New York

SECOND PRINTING

SBN 671-20903-5
Library of Congress Catalog Card Number: 70-161615
Designed by Jack Jaget
Manufactured in the United States of America
By The Book Press Inc., Brattleboro, Vt.

JINK—violent evasive action and reaction to avoid extreme hazard from enemy fire. *Caution*—overreaction by the pilot can result in the loss of the aircraft. Tactical Bulletin 128. June 11, 1967, Eleventh Fighter Command, Southeast Theater; T. A. Bullock, Commanding.

# 1

As the fragments did their deadly dance on the top of the canopy, I kept remembering what Blake had said in that first briefing at Ubon.

I hadn't looked at his gaunt face, the yellow skin, even the bloodless gash that was his mouth. I had been fascinated by the black continents of sweat that formed under his arms, despite the wheezing air conditioning in the Quonset hut.

The soft Virginia voice drawled: "When the fragments bounce in a straight line on the canopy over your head, jink, damn it jink, or you've bought the package."

Like he said, the fragments *ping*ed on the top of the canopy, bisecting it with little flashes of red; then they bounced off erratically like steel balls in a pinball machine.

The fragments turned to green. Just as the word "tracers" registered on my mind, the intercom blasted.

"Jink, Major, jink goddamn it." Automatically I pushed the stick left. The fragments followed, tinkled down the center as smoothly and precisely as a Benny Goodman cadenza.

"Jesus, they're on target," I thought mechanically, and shoved the stick right. The bird moved violently and resentfully. The fragments moved with us, like iron filings in a magnetic experiment I'd once done in high school.

Charley's voice on the intercom screamed:

"Holy Christ, Major, jink!"

"Steady as she goes, Two," I said. I was pleased with the voice that squeezed past the copper taste of fear in my mouth. Just like the Air Force Officers' Guide Book said. Controlled, easy, the habit of command.

But I followed Charley's advice. I put her in a dive.

That's one of the good things about the F-4. With all that armament and the computer, the bitch has got weight. No speed maybe, nothing like the 800 mph the MIGs have. But weight it has, and when you head her over and

7

down, she moves like a keg of beer in a noncom club on Saturday night. Real quick.

We got down below the ridges, down into the black valley, down into the warm dark womb. I saw the flashes over my head—and it took me a moment to realize that it was the AA guns high over the plane.

"How about that," I said idiotically, and then not so idiotically I stayed in the nice black cocoon of the valley that kept us safe.

There was a sudden bright flash of life. Something rammed into my back and I felt pain in my shoulder. I struggled against the belt, reached for the ejection handle, but the shoulder wouldn't move.

My eyes opened. There was a nice black and white picture now—no vivid reds, only the olive drab of an arm with a T-5 stripe on it. The owner of the sleeve was leaning down peering into my face. I heard him say: "Easy on, Major. Better wake up. We're letting down in MacDill in four minutes."

It took me a few seconds to get him and what he was saying into focus, and beyond his head, the bare metal details of the C-140 we were riding in.

"Thanks, Sergeant," I mumbled. Automatically, I reached for a cigarette. He kept his hand on my shoulder.

"No smoking, sir," he said, and I nodded.

"Bad dream?"

"Bad enough," I said. It was true. But the dream wasn't as bad as it really had been those six nights hand running over Min Da, where, as soon as Washington had announced the bombing halt, the bad guys had moved half the AA guns south to cover an infiltration route through the mountains.

The sergeant moved down the cargo ship and I saw him lean down to wake up the others. I blinked a couple of times. I was glad as always the dream was over, but my back hurt. I fumbled behind me. The B-bag was there —so was the helmet. Tho Air Force is efficient, but there's still no way to get a jet helmet into a B-bag, and the helmet

8

is still the only indispensable tool of a trade that these days takes you all over the world.

We came into MacDill. I remembered enough of my days in ATC to make a mental note that if the pilot of the C-140 were one of my kids, I'd eat on his tail a little. It was a kind of hop, skip and bump that he used to bring the ship in. We shuddered to a halt.

The rear door opened—I was home. Not Home—that's a snow-ridged corner of Vermont—just home with a small "h." I went out the door into the humid air of St. Petersburg. The corporal in the mathematically pressed uniform at the bottom of the steps said: "Good evening, sir."

I asked: "What about transportation, Corporal?" and he ignored me and I had an old feeling. I wanted to say: "Don't you know there's a war on?" and then I remembered that would probably be his line.

It wasn't. "It's Sunday night, sir," he said, as if that explained everything, and it did. At a stateside base, everything stops on Friday at 4:00 P.M. just like it does in a well-ordered corporation. Everybody remembers Pearl Harbor but the military.

"Can I get a jeep to Base Ops?"

"Hop in, sir," he said, pointing to a jeep. I did and we cowboyed our way to the Ops building. I looked around the room. I'd spent a year on this base, but I didn't know a soul. I dropped the B-bag and helmet and waited until the well-tailored sergeant got off the phone.

"Got anybody going into town soon, Sergeant?"

"Not a soul, Major. Glad to get you a cab, though."

I sat down to wait. If I was lucky, it might only take half an hour. I debated whether I'd call Anne, then decided after seeing two forty-five on the face of my watch that she'd be dead asleep. What wife with three young kids is up after eleven o'clock?

I told the cabdriver: "Eighty-four-oh-nine Payson Drive." He didn't start the machine; instead he turned around.

"Sorry, bud, I don't know that one," he said. "Can you give me an idea where it is?"

For a moment I was irritated, then I calmed down.

"Yes. Over the causeway, turn left at the Flamingo Country Club and it's the third street on the right after you hit Maplewood Avenue."

"Right," he said. His mouth kept moving, but the words were lost in his clashing start. It was understandable he didn't know Payson Place. It's one of those new developments that pop up like sand crabs all around southern air bases. They're all the same—brand new, badly built with lots of venetian blinds, creaky air conditioning and instant lawns. They've got to be new—there's little time for do-it-yourselfing when you're flying—and by the time the cracks and creaks appear, you've moved on to another state, another base, another mortgage and usually another bedroom.

The cab rocketed to Maplewood and then the driver cautiously felt his way to the third street on the right.

We went down the serpentine street of Payson Village, "where your children can play in safety."

"Pull up here, driver, please," I said.

I paid him off, picked up the B-bag and gear. His headlights as he turned in the driveway next door swung across the neat white sign: "Major John B. McKendrick." I prefer to leave the military rank off, but Anne has a thing about it. So do most of the Air Force wives in developments like ours, so I'd given in.

I walked up the flagstones, instinctively picked up the bike lying on the edge of the lawn and put it near the front door. The house was dark, but the key was under the mat and I slid it into the lock, opened the door gently and stepped into the living room. I reached for the wall light switch, then changed my mind and turned to a small lamp on the end table instead.

The room leaped into view. Everything was pretty much as I remembered it, right down to the toys and clothes and books the kids always left scattered about. Anne is, in many ways, a remarkable girl, but a spic-and-span home-making talent isn't among her virtues.

I felt warm and then noticed that the air conditioning wasn't on. That was odd. Anne's one of those southern girls, northern Florida to be exact, and cool rooms are as much a part of them as fancy sunglasses. I flicked it on and listened. It creaked just like I remembered.

I sat down on the couch and took off the boots. There wasn't any point in waking the kids, I thought. I padded my way into the kitchen, got a tall glass of milk from the refrigerator, and a couple of cookies and went to our bedroom. I pushed the door open softly and listened for her breathing. I could hear nothing. I slipped into the room, moved over to the double bed, put my hand down. I could feeling nothing—and I had a moment of panic. Quickly I put the milk and cookies on the night table and switched on the light. In bewilderment I looked at the empty bed.

Everything seemed normal in the room. Her clothes, as usual, were scattered on the chairs. I got up and went into the kids' rooms. They were empty too. The beds were unmade, the clothing still on the floor where the kids had stepped out of them.

I sat down on Anne's bed and tried to figure it out. She knew I was coming. I'd phoned her three days ago from Saigon—and she'd said nothing then about not being home. Of course it was in the morning, Florida time, when I'd finally got a clear line on which to talk to her. She might have been sleepy, confused; Sunday and Monday sound alike on an overseas hookup. So she'd probably gone up to her mother's in Indian River.

I searched the dressing table in the bedroom for a note, tried the bulletin board on the kitchen wall, the desk in the living room. When she remembered, those were the principal places where Anne left a note.

I looked at the silent phone beside the bed. How about the Jenkinses, our next-door neighbors. They'd know. Or Mary Ellington, Anne's best friend. Tim, her husband, was in Supply. But then I remembered. Calls in the middle of the night to service wives are no kindness. They're only a prelude to a long and agonizing wait for bad news.

The taste of the homecoming was souring in my mouth. The irritation was changing into slow, burning anger. Hell, if Anne wanted to go visit her mother and take the kids, I could understand that. But no note, no message, no nothing? It was the kind of inconsiderate flightiness that had provoked the bitterest of the few quarrels we had had.

I took the milk and dumped it in the sink, dropped the cookies in the garbage. For a moment I thought of cooling my anger in a drink, but I've got out of that habit. I pulled off the flight suit roughly and ducked into the shower. It didn't make me feel any better when I couldn't find clean pajamas, but I threw myself into bed anyway. Before I put the light out, I took another look at the phone. I could call her mother, I thought, and then I said: "The hell with it. It's her loss too."

I was still feeling sorry for myself in the morning and I took my time before I started to try to run down Anne and the kids. Before I left Ubon, I'd promised myself a slow, leisurely breakfast, and I grimly went through the routine of juice, bacon and eggs and toast, carefully washed the dishes and after a shower slipped into slacks and a T-shirt and an old pair of moccasins. Before I went out the back door to talk to Ceil Jenkins, I caught a look at myself in the mirror and then forced a smile over the look of smoldering anger. Neighbors are neighbors and the Jenkinses were good ones—but I knew Anne would never forgive me if I let Ceil know how upset I was to arrive home and find she had gone without a message.

I walked across the back lawn and knocked on the kitchen door. A harried brunette looked out:

"Yes?"

"I'm sorry to disturb you," I smiled, "but is Mrs. Jenkins home?"

"Mrs. Jenkins?" There was a puzzled look on her face. "Oh, you mean the lady who used to live here. I'm sorry. She's left—I think for North Carolina."

"North Carolina?" I echoed. It had a familiar ring to it. Somewhere a memory stirred. Anne had mentioned something about the Jenkinses. I noticed the curious look on the brunette's face.

"Oh, I'm sorry—I'm Major McKendrick," I said. "Your next-door neighbor. I just got back last night from a tour —and I guess my wife, Anne, and I got our signals crossed. She's not home."

A quick look of understanding crossed her face. She gave me a slight smile.

"I'm Maude Friendly," she said. "Captain Friendly's wife. It's happened to us a couple of times—weather, broken aircraft, that kind of thing. I'm sorry, Major, but I don't think I can help you. We moved in only two days ago and I haven't even met your wife. I know the house has been dark since we arrived."

It took me a few minutes to get away from her flood of personal detail. Friendly had come from Craig to Mac-Dill; he was checking out on F-4s. They didn't know where he'd be assigned. We discovered a mutual acquaintance or two and I got away, assuring her that as soon as Anne got back we'd get together for coffee. I retreated to the house.

Mary Ellington's genuine pleasure at my return bubbled right through the telephone receiver. I mentioned that I'd seen Tim in Danang and we'd had dinner together. My impatience mounted when I got trapped into a full report of his health, his job, his prospects, but it was the least I could do. Tim would have done it for me.

"Let me talk to Anne," Mary said then, "She must be up on Cloud Nine this morning."

I hesitated. "That's what I wanted to talk to you about, Mary. She's not home. Neither are the kids. Do you know whether she went up to Indian River?"

"Gosh, John, she might have. I don't know. I haven't seen her for a week."

"You haven't?"

"No. I know she's my best friend and all, but golly, when I heard you were coming home, I got this funny feeling. I know it's silly, but it's the way women are. I felt so happy for her and still so darn envious—and then I didn't drop in because I'd probably get blubbery because Tim isn't coming home for months, and spoil it for Anne."

I told her I understood and then she broke in again.

"John, I'm sure she's at her mother's. Give her a call right this minute, you hear? She'll hate herself for missing her first night with you. But now that you're back for good, it will be all right."

"Sure, Mary, I'll call. Right away."

"And John—"

"Yes?"

"As soon as she gets back, you all come over, you hear?"

"Sure, Mary, almost as soon as she gets back."

She chuckled. "You fellows. You've only got one thing on your mind. Thank the Lord."

I was smiling when I hung up. I looked up Anne's mother's number and dialed it.

Her birdlike voice came through the receiver.

"John, how nice to hear from you after all this time. How are you?"

"Fine, Grace." She's one of that strange breed of women who find the words "Mother" and "Grandmother" abhorrent.

"Anne must be happy," she said. "And I'm sure the children are thrilled."

"You mean, she's not with you, Grace?"

"Why no, John, isn't she there?"

I forced a laugh. "No, she isn't. I guess she got her signals crossed. Neither she nor the kids are here. The first place I thought of was yours. But perhaps she took the kids and went down to visit the Waldrons." June Waldron is an old college friend of Anne's—and I knew Grace liked her.

"Goodness, John, I don't know what young mothers are like these days. I know I wouldn't go away after Henry had been gone a year."

"Just a mixup, I guess, Grace. Well, I won't keep you. I've got to check into the base in a few minutes. You know, reports, that kind of thing."

It was a white lie. My orders were cut for Randolph, and MacDill couldn't care less about one of their former pilots, but I wanted to avoid any possibility that Grace would think I was worried.

I got off the phone quickly. Grace isn't sure what the Air Force is all about, but she's convinced I spend most of my days snarled up in red tape. She's more than half right, come to think of it.

I sat staring at the phone. The anger had gone, leaving only bewilderment. Anne was careless about notes, but this was ridiculous.

Suddenly I heard the kitchen door open and I sprang up, a feeling of relief and new anger surging through me. I was there in half a dozen steps, ready to kiss her and kick her. I stopped abruptly in the door. It wasn't Anne, it was Hattie, the huge black daylady, who came once a week.

She grinned at me. "Well, if it isn't the Mister! My, my, it's good to see you back in one piece."

She caught the expression on my face.

"Anything wrong, Major?" she asked anxiously. "You don't look happy like a man ought to, returning to a pretty wife and three fine kids."

"I don't know, Hattie. I got back last night and Mrs. McKendrick and the kids aren't here. Got any idea where she is? Did she tell you anything about where she was going?"

"My goodness, is that all that's bothering you?" she said with a broad smile. "Gosh, Major, you've been living with that little girl long enough to know she takes something into her head, she's bang and gone! Probably run up to her mother's—or one of her friends."

"She's not at her mother's, Hattie. I called there. I called Mrs. Ellington too; she doesn't know anything either."

"That don't mean much, Major," she said firmly. "I'm sure she'll pop up sometime today. Now just don't you worry. And don't you plan on staying around here moping. Go out and go fishing or something. I swear to goodness, this house is a mess. Nobody in this house ever heard of hooks or closets. Come on now, git."

She made sense. I'm not very big for fishing, but now that I thought of it, a few hours dunking a line in the channel off the causeway didn't sound like a bad idea. I went out in the garage, rescued the fishing tackle box. I couldn't find one of my rods and truth to tell, with two growing boys, didn't expect to. I got one of Sean's. It wasn't much good, but it was an excuse to stand in the sun and drop a line in the water.

I solved the transportation problem with a bike Anne had bought. She's always on an exercise-dieting kick, trying to fight off the effects of three babies on a size-four figure.

I heard Hattie come to the door.

"You want a sandwich or something to take with you, Major?"

"No thanks," I said. "I'll pick up a hot dog or a hamburger."

I swung a leg over the bike, then felt her hand on my arm.

"Major, it's mighty good to have you back," she said. "Time this house got a good shaping up. Those are fine kids you got, but it takes a man to learn them their p's and q's."

When you sire two boys and an active little girl, you get to be expert at untangling fishing lines, but it still took me the better part of half an hour on the bridge to get the fishing line straightened out. I put on a worm, climbed up on the parapet and dropped the hook in the water.

Nothing happened and that was great with me. The skyline of St. Pete had changed since I'd been away. More white blocks of concrete, and even though I couldn't see them, I knew that more highways had been opened up in another futile effort to avoid the mounting arteriosclerosis of traffic. But nothing had affected the bay—a broad expanse of sun-dappled water, broken only by an occasional rowboat and a couple of outboards.

I half-dozed for an hour and then realized I was ravenously hungry. I packed the gear, put the tackle box in the basket and headed off the bridge.

I'd been to the little roadside shack a half-dozen times maybe. The guy at the grill—I guess he was the Sam of Sam's Sandy Shores Shack—was just getting ready for the lunch business. The great big tattoos on his arms had always fascinated my kids.

"Hi," he said, "what'll it be?"

"A couple of hot dogs. Mustard—and if you got the time, toast the rolls."

"Time I got, fella," he said cheerfully. He looked at me more closely. "Haven't seen you around lately."

"Been traveling," I said. He snapped his fingers.

"Got it," he said triumphantly. "It's McKendrick, ain't it? What is it now, major or captain?"

"Major," I said. "But how'd you know? I haven't been here all that often."

"Easy," he said. "You're the one with the kids, the red-headed ones, aren't you?"

"That's right, two boys and a girl."

"They've been here, maybe six, eight times a month. Nice kids, good manners, polite as you please."

It's always the way—hoodlums at home, Little Lord Fauntleroys away, but I was pleased nevertheless.

He held the toasted rolls on a fork for my inspection.

" 'Bout right, Major?" he asked. "How come they're not with you today—the kids, I mean?"

I hesitated, but before I could say something, he added: "That's right. They're away. I remember now."

"That's kids for you," I said quietly for fear I'd shut off the flow of information. "Always spilling the family secrets."

"No sir, Major," he said vigorously, "they didn't tell me. I saw them going."

He turned away at that moment to give the hot dogs a couple of turns. "You know this place, Major. Not much goes on. You get in the habit of watching the highway, looking at people, trying to figure them out."

"Figure them out? How?"

"You know, honeymooners, retired folks, what are they, where are they going. So I noticed your kids and the missus a couple of days ago. Frankly speaking, Major, they surprised me."

"How's that?" I asked, reaching for the hot dogs on the paper plate he shoved at me.

"Coffee, tea or milk?" he asked. "I don't really carry no tea, but I saw an airline commercial and that's what the hostess says, so I say it. Funny thing, nobody wants tea."

"How about that?" I said. "A Coke, I think."

He opened the cap, slid the bottle across to me, then folded his arms and leaned one hip against the counter.

"Like I said, Major," he said as if he hadn't interrupted himself, "I was a little surprised."

"Like how?" I asked.

"If you'll excuse the remark, Major, that blue station wagon you folks have ain't exactly a Jaguar, and when it was passing here, it was going like the hammers of Hell. Maybe seventy-five—and as for me I don't like mothers driving little kids at that kind of speed. Then I noticed it wasn't your wife driving. There was a man at the wheel, another one alongside of him was talking to your wife. By the way, who was the clown driving?"

"I don't know. What'd he look like?"

"Ordinary—ordinary sports shirt, long hair though, not hippie hair but long like a surfer. I thought he was young —kind of pink, reddish hair."

"Can't place him right off," I said evasively. Anne's got a lot of cousins in Florida—could be one of them. "Maybe, if you could tell me something about the other fellow—"

He shook his head. "Sorry, just a guy, maybe a little on the Spick side. Anyway, if you catch up with that first guy, the red-pinky-haired guy, you tell him watch that speed, okay?"

"I sure will," I said. I looked at my watch. I suddenly wanted to get home. "Gosh, it's later than I thought," I said. "I've got to run. Thanks a lot, though. Be seeing you."

"Great, Major," he said. I got on the bike. "Hey," he said. "Take that other hot dog with you. You can ride with one hand and eat it on the way home."

One hand or no, I couldn't get down another bite and I dumped it into the trash basket on one of the little picnic sites that face the beaches.

Sam had confused me more than ever. First, I didn't know any long-haired, red-pinky-haired man; second, Anne knows I'm a fanatic about high speeds—and after years on tightly patroled bases, she's got the message. Anyway, the blue Ford station wagon is a clunker, running more on hope than health. They were heading north, yet Anne's mother hadn't heard from her. The Waldrons lived down Sarasota way, so that was wrong too. I found myself pumping furiously on the bike to get home, but for the life of me, I couldn't figure out what I was going to do when I got there.

I propped the bike against the garage wall and stepped into the house. The same appalling quiet met me at the door. Mechanically, I went to the cabinet, poured a finger of Scotch in the glass, got two cubes from the icebox, took the drink and sat on the end of the sofa.

I took a sip of the drink. It tasted lousy. I took another sip and then I knew why. The Scotch couldn't cut the copper taste of fear in my mouth—the same feeling I'd had when the guns of Min Da were zeroing in on me. I let into the light of day the thought that had been skittering through the back of my brain.

"My wife and three kids are missing," I said aloud. "My wife and three kids."

# 2

It was easy to dislike Lieutenant Kennedy at first glance. It got easier the longer you were exposed to him.

I opened the door when he rang the bell.

"Major McKendrick?" he asked. "Lieutenant Kennedy. G-2."

"Come in," I said.

Then the son of a bitch actually came in, stood at attention, his cap carefully under his arm, waiting for my command.

"Oh, for Christ's sake, sit down," I growled.

"Thank you, sir," he said.

He gave the room that inspector-general look and I remembered the time I'd been commanding a tiny Japanese base and the white gloves separated the men from those who got demerits. Kennedy didn't like development houses and he didn't like bad or indifferent housekeepers like Anne, even with a twice weekly maid, and it was a cinch that in his whole life he hadn't picked up after a young son.

I lit a cigarette and he refused one with an air that I was a traitor to the surgeon general's office.

"Okay, you called me," I said. "What gives?"

"How long have you been out of the country?" he asked.

"Thirteen months, eleven days," I said.

"That explains it," he said.

"Explains what?"

"You went out of channels."

"Excuse me, Lieutenant," I said bitterly. "I'm not accustomed to losing a wife and three children every day in the week. I got maybe excited."

"Don't get excited now, sir," he said patiently. "We have a lot of ground to cover. Are you ready, sir?"

I looked at him, at the crease in the sixty-dollar trousers, the handmade blouse, the nonregulation, nondusty shoes. I couldn't imagine Lieutenant Kennedy out of channels, ever. Otherwise he'd lose his option to pose for those posters the AF tries to get up on the college bulletin boards. "Go first class all the way—fly there with the United States Air Force." He'd have the helmet tucked under his arm, the blue eyes in his hawlike face looking at a nonexistent horizon, on twenty-four-hour alert for the enemy.

"Tell me, Lieutenant," I asked, "whose side are you on?"

"Oh Christ," he said, "don't you jockey types ever change? Is it always good guys, bad guys?"

"Always," I said.

"Okay, if that's the way you want it, let me take you through the drill," he said. "You got back from Vietnam last night."

"Thailand," I said.

"Thailand then. You tell me you definitely told your wife you'd be here Sunday night, late. She's not here, your kids are not here. So why make a federal case? Could be she's visiting relatives, friends."

"I checked her mother, her best friend, the next-door neighbors, Lieutenant. Nobody knows a thing. Except the man at the hot dog stand. He saw them going north with two men in the car."

"So you said. What about notes?"

"None, but look for yourself," I said shortly.

"I will."

He did a good job on the living room—then moved into the bedroom. I thought of another drink but discarded the idea quickly. I get nothing out of liquor and I'm not unusual among fighter pilots. There are still a few clowns who do the World War II dawn patrol bit, but most of us are beyond thirty—and the reflexes show alcohol too quickly.

Kennedy was right. I had gone out of channels. The reason was stupidly simple. Riding back from Sam's Sandy Shores Shack, I got scared. So I got into uniform, caught a cab out to the base and tried to find someone who could help.

It isn't as easy as it sounds. A base like MacDill is really two kinds of installation. The great bulk of its activity is final fighter-pilot training. In a curious way, these people are on the base and yet they're not of it. They're on a six-day-a-week push, push, push schedule. For the better part of nine months, they're hitting the flight line at five twenty in the morning—and it's an easy day when they get back home before nine at night. Between those early morning hours and the dark, there's not time for socializing. The permanent base people are there—you know that—they're names on a door or on a mimeographed bulletin. For Anne and me, the only people on the base who we really got to know were the people in the hospital. With three little kids, that's normal. Occasionally in the

21

nine months, I'd run across an acquaintance or two from a former station—but they were usually on the same kind of training grind, and beyond "Whatever happened to Joe?" and "We must get together one of these nights," that was it. It sounds like a tough life, but that's the only way you can cram the essentials in lifetaking and lifesaving into that short a period.

But I went to the base anyway. I didn't know what I was going to do, but I knew I couldn't sit around the house worrying. Then I met Halloran—Sergeant Halloran of the Air Police—and I thought my problems were over. How he ever got an Irish name like Halloran I'll never know. He's about six feet, 210 and black. He got into the MPs during World War II, decided to stay in and has been with it ever since.

We'd met a couple of weeks after I'd gotten to MacDill the first time. I got home early one night for a change and Anne was wringing her hands. Shane, our six-year-old, still hadn't come home from school and she was worried. We were about to start phoning around when the Air Police car pulled up. It was Halloran. He'd found Shane wandering around the base, looking for me, and decided to bring the boy home himself, thinking to save me an extra trip back. He explained to Anne he was on his way home anyway, and yes ma'am, a cup of coffee would go down mighty fine right now.

He ended up of course with the kids on his lap and invited them to visit the base, where he'd give them the full treatment. I had no doubt he'd be able to show them more than I could.

When I walked into the Air Police station on the base he was sitting at a desk, enjoying a very large, very black, very contraband Cuban cigar. He looked at me, his eyes widening in recognition, and he got up from his chair.

"Major McKendrick, nice to see you back, sir," he said.

I stuck out my hand and after a moment's hesitation he shook it.

"Nice to be back, Sergeant," I said. I noticed the other

APs looking at me with curiosity. "Can I see you a moment, alone, Sergeant?"

He frowned, then said easily: "Sure thing, sir. Time for a coffee break anyhow."

He chose a table in the corner of the cafeteria with lots of room between us and the few other people in the room.

"Well, Major, what's it all about? Shane gone wandering again?"

I filled him in on the story, including the hot dog man. The shrewd eyes never left my face.

"So?" he said. "What can we do?"

"Could you—" I hesitated—"could you check the local police, the hospital"—I stopped and then got the word out —"the morgue?"

He looked at me with narrowed eyes.

"Your orders are cut for San Antonio, right?"

I nodded.

"Then you know," he said slowly, "that properly speaking this isn't a MacDill matter. Rightly, you ought to get in touch with Randolph. You're their baby."

He knew as well as I did that I couldn't get in touch with Randolph. The Air Force is a peculiar institution; they don't like people who make waves—who go running to the local police with a scare report about a Missing Air Force Wife and a Couple of Kids. The incident would find its way into a fitness report with a great big question mark.

"Hell, Sergeant, you know the score on that."

"Rightly, Major, I ought to clear this with my boss, Lieutenant Hutchinson."

I nodded and he smiled.

"But rightly speaking, Lieutenant Hutchinson at this precise minute"—he looked at his watch—"is three quarters of the way to Jacksonville to speak to a meeting of the Rotary Club. So he couldn't help. Let me think this over for a minute, Major."

He closed his eyes and puffed thoughtfully on his cigar.

"Tell you what, Major. You stick around here for a few minutes. Go buy yourself a drink or something at the

Officers' Club. I'll make arrangements to leave early; then I'll make a phone call or two."

I was about to suggest that was a lot of trouble for him, but he held up a big hand to shush me.

"Look, Major, we don't want a phone call like this one going through the base switchboard. Lots of big ears in a place like this. Now don't worry. We'll get things started in a hurry."

I hitched up to the bar in the club and toyed with a beer for a few minutes. When Halloran came in, he gave me a nod and I left with him.

He didn't say much in the car until we were almost home. Then he asked: "This red-pinky-haired joker the hot dog man told you about—was he anyone you met before— maybe a relative of your wife's?"

"No, I don't think so, Sergeant. Her stepbrother's got black hair. But you know how it is. Moving around like I do. I might have met him somewhere, but I haven't been able to remember it if I did."

"Don't sweat it, sir," he said. "Just bury it in the back of your head. If you remember, it'll come popping up out of your subconscious."

We turned into my street and just as we spotted my house, I saw a car in my driveway. I jabbed Halloran in the ribs.

"There's a car in my driveway. Look, Sergeant!"

"Yes, Major, I know."

"You know! What do you mean you know?"

"It's my car," he said. "I asked my wife to bring it over.

"But why?" I was genuinely puzzled.

"You're going to need transportation," he said. "You can have my car for a couple of days. Okay?" He looked straight ahead through the windshield.

"Sergeant—" I started.

"Like I said before, Major, don't sweat it. It's done."

Mrs. Halloran was tall, thin and poised. She refused my invitation to come into the house; she said she'd wait in the Air Police car.

Halloran didn't waste any time. He picked up the phone, dialed a number, listened, then spoke: "Captain Hernandez, please. Sergeant Halloran."

I heard an answering voice come through the receiver.

With a big wink at me, Halloran broke into a torrent of Spanish. It was too rapid for me to follow, but then I've never got past the "*como se llama*" stage myself. At one point, Halloran stopped and asked me: "Your car, Major. I know it's a Ford station wagon, but what year?"

"1964."

"License plate?"

"I'm sorry. I don't know the new number. It's been a year since I left, remember?"

"No trouble, Major."

He went back to the Spanish, listened to the voice on the other end, said: "*Muchas gracias, mi Capitán.*"

I tried to mask my anxiety with a casual question.

"I didn't know you spoke Spanish so well, Sergeant."

He grinned. "It's a put-on, Major. Captain Hernandez speaks English better than both of us."

"But where did you learn it?"

He widened his eyes innocently. "Don't you read the recruiting literature, Major? The Armed Forces Institute— 'where you can get an education while you're serving your country.' Those nights at the Air Police desk can be long and dull." His eyes twinkled. "To tell the truth, I kind of got pushed into it. Angela, my wife, got her master's at Columbia."

"What did Captain Hernandez say?"

The answer was direct and businesslike. "I gave him a description of your wife and children and the car. He'll check the obvious places, reports of accidents, hospitals, the works. I told him your situation. He'll do the job discreetly. That takes longer, but he knows the Air Force. He'll call you here in a couple of hours. After that, we'll see. In the meantime, a piece of well-meaning advice: Don't worry. These things rarely turn out as bad as we think."

"But if Hernandez finds nothing, what do we do, Sergeant?"

"Time enough for that later." He wrote his phone number down. "Get me here, anytime."

It was the sheerest bad luck that Halloran's efforts got him in trouble. Hernandez made his checks discreetly enough. He was waiting for a rundown of county auto accidents, when he got called out on an urgent nasty job. A cop had been killed during a suspected break-in and Hernandez had to cover the crime personally. He asked an assistant to make the rest of my calls. The assistant decided to report to Halloran instead of to me. In view of the urgency of the case, he called the Air Police on the base. Then came the hassle on the phone. A young corporal hearing the slightly Spanish accent of Hernandez' assistant, gave him a hard time. Wrapped in a huff, the policeman insisted on talking to the officer on duty and the fat was in the fire. Halloran was hauled back to the base, where he had to tell the whole story, and that brought Lieutenant Kennedy to my bedroom.

He came out of the bedroom now.

"No note," he said. He prowled the rest of the house for a few minutes; he even went to the refrigerator and poked around there.

"I don't think you'll find a note in the icebox, Lieutenant," I said sarcastically.

"Um?" he said absently.

He came back in the living room and sat down across from me. The frown lines were deep in his forehead.

"Major, I hope you don't think I was prying. But I noticed your wife's jewel box. Isn't that rather a lot of jewelry?"

"Oh that. Yes, I think it is a lot—but for a couple of years in Japan, Anne ran a boutique as part of the PX, and one of the items they stocked was jewelry. Like every woman, she can't resist wholesale prices."

"Wholesale?"

"Yes, Anne did all the buying for the boutique. Most of

26

the stuff was marked up about twenty per cent. When something came in from Thailand or Bangkok or Hong Kong, something she particularly liked, she sold it to herself wholesale. She figured that sort of paid her back for all the work she was doing—tending the shop, et cetera."

"I see. I'll have to talk to her when she gets back. She's got exquisite taste and I've got a girl back in Boston."

"Fine, Lieutenant. Now, how about my problem?"

"I've got to get back to the base and get things started. Quietly, you understand. We don't want any scare stories in the local papers, you know. Say, I've got an idea."

He looked around the house.

"You haven't eaten, have you?" he asked.

"No."

"Well, how about going out to the club with me? I'll get the wheels in motion; then while we're eating, if I get any more ideas I'll have you right at hand and you can give me any further information I may need. It might speed things up a bit."

After his last line, I had no choice. I slipped into a clean shirt, found a subdued sports jacket and joined him at the door. I started to open the door of Halloran's car.

"No," he said sharply. "We'll go in my car."

It was almost a command and I raised my eyebrows.

"I meant, Major, there's not much point in taking two cars. I'll drop you off or we can get one of the men at the base to give you a lift." It made sense so I climbed in with him.

We hadn't been driving more than a minute when he flicked on the radio. The inevitable Latin beat blasted out at us. He turned it down. "Dreadful sound," he said, "but at least it's not rock 'n' roll."

He said only one thing more, and that as we pulled into the parking lot of the Officers' Club.

"Was it successful?" he asked.

"Was what successful?"

"The boutique. The one your wife, Anne, opened."

I looked at him and shrugged. "Very. I think the shop

27

earned something like $22,000 profit in a year."

He whistled. "Very nice for you both, I should think."

"We didn't make a dime. The profit went to the base recreation fund."

"You don't say?" The note of disbelief was clear. "That was very generous of your wife."

"Generosity had nothing to do with it," I said sharply. "You know regulations as well as I do."

"That's right," he said matter-of-factly. "I do."

# 3

Kennedy led the way through the main dining room. He said over his shoulder: "The grill's likely to be quieter." He ploughed ahead as if he didn't care whether I minded or not.

The grill had the usual complement of fake oak beams, dusty World War II relics, solitary eaters and drinkers and the inevitable quartet who looked like they'd been there through lunch and maybe breakfast.

Kennedy was angling for the corner of the grill and he stopped so abruptly I bumped into him.

His way was barred by a vintage World War II type of colonel, lean, ice-eyed with a crew cut so flat you could land a T-28 on it. He was wearing the trade school ring, of course, and when he invited us to sit down and have a drink, it wasn't an invitation. It was unthinkable to him that we'd say no. The colonel's table was already set for three; apparently both of his guests had gone to the loo.

The black plastic label on his blouse pocket said: "Colonel F. M. Sanders." His raised eyebrows asked me what I wanted. I said Scotch. Kennedy nodded ditto. Sanders waved a hand negligently and the drinks appeared so fast it was like a television show.

Sanders gave me no more than a glance—I do that to

full colonels. He concentrated on Kennedy and it was clear they knew each other well. They replayed a recent wedding they'd both attended, exchanged some very in stuff, and then it was my turn.

"Just back, Major?" Sanders asked.

"Last night, sir."

"Ubon, wasn't it?"

"Yes sir, thirteen months."

Out of the corner of my eye I could see Kennedy rather elaborately surveying the room and pretending to take no interest in the conversation.

I didn't like the conversation. Sanders knew too much about me for a chance drink in the bar. He went on: "F-4s standing up?"

"Yes sir. We had a performance ratio of 3.7."

I watched him. That isn't classified, but it's not general knowledge. Incidentally, it's a hell of a good performance ratio and he should have been surprised by it. He passed it by.

I turned to Kennedy.

"Shouldn't we move on, Lieutenant? We don't want to keep the colonel from his guests."

Sanders said abruptly: "There's nothing private about this dinner, Major. Just a few friends. Like to have you with us." Kennedy picked up the menu. That was my cue that the matter was settled. But I was nettled.

"I don't think I caught where you're stationed," I said.

"I don't recall saying, Major," Sanders said.

He looked over my shoulder. Two civilians were standing behind us.

The colonel didn't get up. He pointed at the beefy one in a loud sports jacket: "Major McKendrick, meet Tom Logan. The other gentleman is Sol Jacobs. Sit down, gentlemen; the major and lieutenant are joining us for dinner."

We shook hands, shuffled places and I found myself directly across from Sanders and between the two civilians. Another round of drinks appeared without a comment and we spent all of two minutes acceding to the colonel's choice of sirloins on the rare side, a Roquefort salad and home fries.

Logan politely asked where I'd been, I told him and he said the usual polite things about how tough it must have been. I denied it. Jacobs, who'd been busily working on his salad, laid down his fork and said abruptly:

"Get into Hong Kong often, Major?"

The others sat a little bit more erect at the question.

"Twice," I said.

"Hear there are some great bargains," said Jacobs. He didn't seem interested in pursuing the subject but went back to his lettuce. We spent the rest of the dinner discussing Thai silks, Phillipine lace, Hong Kong tailors and inevitably the high price of everything in the States. We came to the conclusion reached in every Officer's Club around the world: If you only had the money, you could make a hell of a lot of good deals in foreign countries.

The colonel ordered brandy. I passed, so did Jacobs. Logan ordered an ale. When Kennedy ordered brandy, too, I got nudgy.

"I'd like to get along, Lieutenant." I turned to Sanders. "The lieutenant and I have a little business to do, sir," I said, "if you don't mind?"

"What business is that, Major?" No hint of the rudeness of the question showed in the ice blue eyes.

I dropped my own ice cubes into the comment. "It's a personal matter, sir."

"No problem," he said. "I'm an old hand at trouble." He slid the ID card across the table. It had the usual stamps, endorsements, the passport-type photo. It said simply: "Sanders, F. M., Col., USAF, Intelligence." It gave the assignment as Washington, D.C.

I didn't pick up the ID card, just looked him in the eye.

"As I've indicated," I said, "it's personal, Colonel." I put my hands on the table, ready to shove off.

"Hold it, Major," said Kennedy. "As you've gathered, this meeting isn't exactly unplanned. I called the colonel about your problem before I left for your house. He offered to help. Since he was having dinner with Mr. Logan and Mr. Jacobs, I took the liberty of taking him up on the offer. Mr. Logan is with the Federal Bureau of Investigation; Mr. Jacobs is with the inspector general's office."

He turned to Sanders. "Your office or mine, sir?"

"Yours is fine, Lieutenant. Shall we go along, Major McKendrick?"

Kennedy's office was strictly functional—gray files, gray desk, gray chairs, gray carafe—with one exception: one of those Harvard so-called captain's chairs, complete with the seal of the university and the motto in Hebrew. The colonel started to sit down in that one, took a look and changed his mind. He sat behind the desk, Logan draped himself over the file, Kennedy sat in the Harvard chair, Jacobs dragged a chair from the next office and I stood. I could feel the anger making my collar tighter.

"Well, Major," the colonel said easily, "what's the problem?"

"McKendrick, J. B., Major, United States Air Force, Serial Number 123768, sir," I said.

"Now that's no way to react to a nice friendly offer, boy," said Logan. "All the colonel wants to do is help, he said that."

I took two swift strides to the filing cabinet, caught him by the tie and twisted it.

"Listen, you Irish sonofabitch, if you want to find yourself on your butt, say 'boy' to me once more. I spent three years in Selma, Alabama. I didn't like the word then, I don't like it now."

He took two big red hands, caught my wrists and bent them like they were pieces of rigatoni.

"Easy, Major, easy." He didn't let go of the hands but turned to Sanders. "Put him in the picture, Colonel. It might make this faster."

Sanders turned to Kennedy. "The file, please."

Sanders took the manila folder from Kennedy and opened it. "Okay, Major, here it is. According to your story, you returned after thirteen months in Ubon in Thailand. You were attached to the 81st Fighter Squadron. You flew 152 missions as a squadron commander, were shot down once, received the Air Medal with two clusters. Right?"

"Your story, sir," I said tightly.

He turned back to the folder.

"In the course of your present tour of duty, you were out of Thailand some fourteen times, on leave or temporarily detached. Right?"

"Same story, sir."

"We wish to question you about those fourteen times, Major."

"We, sir?" I asked.

"We," he said. "Mr. Logan, Mr. Jacobs, Lieutenant Kennedy and myself.

I'd been racking my brains during the reading of the file, and most of it came back to me.

"May I respectfully refer you, Colonel, to Article 21, Section D, of the Articles of War?"

Sanders looked at me with new interest.

"Let me see if I can quote correctly, Major," he said. " 'No member of the Armed Forces of the United States of America shall be forced to testify against himself, until and when he shall be notified of the crime or crimes of which he has been accused, and he shall at all times have the privilege of counsel, and of confronting the witnesses to the alleged crime or crimes.' Correct, Major?"

"Very good, sir," I said.

"There is however, Major," Kennedy said mildly, "another section from the Code of Conduct that seems applicable. I quote: 'It shall be the duty of an officer of the Armed Forces of the United States to cooperate in any and all endeavors of the higher military authorities, when such authorities shall have reason to believe that the military laws or the laws of the United States of America or any of its political subdivisions shall have been deemed to have been violated. Failure to cooperate fully and in good conscience shall subject the officer to a general court-martial.' "

Sanders looked amused. "Hobson's choice, Major, isn't it?"

"No sir," I said. "I'll stick to Section 21A. In the phrase of my crew chief, screw yourself. Sir."

The mouth tightened.

"That comment may be injudicious, Major. Let me, as our British friends say, put you in the picture. We want some information from you. We think it's vital for the security of the Air Force. We intend to get it—and we don't want any smartassed plane jockey making it difficult. Got that?"

"Blow it," I said bluntly. It was a pleasure to see the anger rise in the colonel's pale face.

It was Jacobs' turn to pour some oil on the troubled waters.

He went over, sat on the corner of the colonel's desk and said: "Take it easy, Major. We really are trying to help." He handed me his ID card, and true enough, it said: "Inspector General's Office, Investigator, Field Staff."

"Okay, Major, now look at this." He handed me a letter. It was signed: "J. W. Hanscome, Brigadier General, Randolph Air Force Base." The message was blunt. It instructed Major J. B. McKendrick to assist Mr. Jacobs of the inspector general's office generally and to give such other assistance as Mr. Jacobs required to cooperate in an investigation of paramount interest to the Air Forces.

"Get it clear now, Major?" asked Jacobs in a gentle voice. "Your commanding officer requests—notice he doesn't order —you to assist us. Like us, he wants everything simple."

I turned to Sanders.

"I'll have that brandy now," I said. "The one you offered."

It can't have been the first time he'd run a star chamber session in Kennedy's office. Without taking his eyes off me, he opened the lower right-hand drawer and pulled out a bottle of Pedro Domecq Three Vines. Like magic, four glasses appeared on the desk and four large dollops were poured.

He saluted me, silently, and said: "Shall we get at it, Major?"

"If you're ready, sir."

He put his hand across the desk and I looked at it blankly. Kennedy rose, fished in his watch pocket and laid a ring in the palm of Sanders' hand. Sanders took it between his thumb and his forefinger, held it up to the light and thrust it at me:

"Recognize that, Major?"

I looked at it closely, held it up to the light. Both Jacobs and Logan were right at my shoulders.

"Yes sir," I told Sanders, "I bought it in Cambodia— Pnompenh, to be exact." I screwed up my eyes, trying to be precise about the date. "I bought it on February 28, 1968, had it gift-wrapped, sent it by registered mail from the post office in Ubon on March 11, 1968. The postage was $1.32. It was a gift to my wife on our ninth wedding anniversary."

"Thank you, Major," said Jacobs. "You have an excellent memory. May I ask why you remember those dates so exactly?"

I looked at him a little bitterly.

"Ever been away from a young wife and three kids, Mr. Jacobs? For more than a year? I can assure you, when you have, exact dates become pretty important."

"It figures," he said. "Can you also remember what you paid for it?"

"Yes sir, to the penny," I said. "It came to $73.16 green."

"Green?"

"Green, Mr. Jacobs. That's American money. You remember we now pay the Armed Forces in scrip," I said, and added sarcastically: "Or doesn't the inspector general's office know that if the troops get American money, it could upset the local currency?"

"I'm sorry, Major," he said, "I should have remembered. Can you think how much that is in Cambodian money?"

"Forty-one hundred and sixty riels, give or take a few."

He looked at me intently, then slowly pulled a piece of notepaper from his pocket. He read it, then looked over its edge at me.

"Major, I have here a note I took on the telephone less

34

than an hour and a half ago. It is an exact transcript of a number given me by Mr. Arnold Johnson, vice president of Haverford's in St. Petersburg. Are you familiar with the name of the store?"

"Yes sir. It's a jewelry store in St. Pete. Too expensive for my tastes, though."

He held the ring in his hand.

"Will you examine the ring, Major, again?"

I took it. "It looks like the one I sent Anne." I felt the dawn of peril but didn't know why.

"Major," he said, "I did not tell Mr. Johnson where that ring came from—that it had been found deep in a pile of lingerie in your wife's bedroom. I merely asked Mr. Johnson to give me an appraisal of the ring's worth."

He paused, then said slowly after a glance at the paper: "Major, in the opinion of Mr. Johnson, that ring is worth approximately $33,000 on the American market. It is, in his opinion, a superb Colombian emerald in a crude Cambodian gold setting."

# 4

I held out my hand and Jacobs dropped the ring into my palm. It still looked like an oversized piece of costume jewelry.

"No possible mistake?" I asked.

"None."

I flipped the jewel back on the desk.

"So what's it got to do with me?"

"You tell us," said Sanders. I knew then for sure I wasn't going to make colonel. You either have those steely blue eyes that pin the victim to the wall or you don't. "It's not every Air Force major who can buy his wife a $33,000 emerald."

"I didn't," I said shortly. "I bought my wife a seventy-three-dollar piece of costume jewelry. It's your story that it's worth thirty-three grand. I've got a receipt to prove what I paid. You remember, don't you, Colonel, that when you send a gift through Customs there's got to be a declaration of value?" I had my fingers crossed when I said it. Maybe Anne still did have the receipt. It was a little unlikely. Most times she mislays the monthly telephone bill, but I figured the bluff was worth it.

I pulled a chair up to the desk, took out a cigarette, lit it and crossed my legs.

"Now, Colonel Sanders, if you don't mind an old Air Force expression, let's get the show on the road. What's this all about? What's the emerald got to do with my wife and kids? Where are my wife and kids?"

"You tell us, Major," he said coldly.

I gave him icy eye for icy eye and stood up. "I guess you want to play games, Colonel," I said. "I don't. I've got a real problem on my hands. My wife and kids are worth a hell of a lot more to me than your lousy ring. You want to help? Great. You want to be cute? Forget it!"

I turned to the door. The FBI type and Kennedy moved closer, as if to prevent my exit.

I said to Logan: "You *are* with the FBI?"

Just like in the movies, he flipped out the wallet, with the badge, the identification card with his picture on it.

"Okay," I said. "I want to report a kidnaping. If I read the papers right, a kidnaping's the Bureau's baby, isn't it?"

"It is, Major," he said agreeably, "but there's a hitch. The Bureau doesn't know that a kidnaping's actually taken place."

I felt the anger surge through me and for a moment I thought of throwing a punch at him; then I remembered how easily he had handled me at the file cabinet.

"My wife is missing—so are my three children. That makes it a kidnaping in my book."

"You're being a little hasty, Major. Before the FBI can move in on an alleged kidnaping, we have to have a little more evidence than we have right now. For example, a ransom note. There's another little hitch. People don't kidnap other people unless they have some way of knowing that the ransom can and will be paid by the relatives of the victim. Who'd want to kidnap the wife and kids of an Air Force officer who's up to his ass in debt, who can't even afford a better car than a 1964 Ford station wagon?"

I chewed on that for a moment. They had obviously checked me out with the local Retail Credit Bureau. While I hadn't had time to get the bad news about our finances from Anne, I could only hope that he was right; that I was only up to my ass in debt and not in over my head.

"She's missing, dammit; so are the kids," I said stubbornly. "If she isn't kidnaped, where is she?"

"There's always another man," he said with a knowing grin.

It was a lucky punch and I couldn't do it again in a month of Sundays, but I caught him flush on the corner of the mouth and he stumbled backward over Kennedy's feet and went down.

Kennedy was all over me in a flash and so was the scrawny Jacobs and they had me back in my chair in seconds. Sanders hadn't moved a muscle, nor had he lost the look of distaste he'd had on his face ever since we got into the office.

Logan got off the floor, dusted the back of his shiny blue serge pants, stuck his hand out and said: "Sorry, Major, I deserved that. I was only making a theoretical point."

"Sit down, Mr. Logan," Sanders said icily. "Now that the dramatics are over, perhaps we can get to the matter at hand."

Jacobs coughed apologetically. "Maybe we could give him a fill-in, Colonel?" He got the usual Sanders glare; then the Colonel looked at me as if he saw me for the first time.

"Okay, McKendrick. We'll give you as much as you're allowed to know. This matter is under tight security."

The field-grade types always use "security," implying that the nation's future is at stake, when what they really mean is that you're too stupid to be told the whole story. They did the same thing back at Ubon and I lost a lot of good young men because they didn't get to know where the traps were on a "routine mission."

Sanders tapped an unlit cigarette on the back of his thumbnail.

"For some time, the Air Force has been hearing rumors of a smuggling operation, working out of the Far East. It started, of course, in Vietnam and it's been spreading. I'm sure this is no surprise to you."

It wasn't. There's always a lot of talk in air bases about smuggling operations. It started way back in World War II. A lot of gold, it was said, was smuggled out of the Far East, over the Hump, with Air Force types taking a piece of the action. It's worse now, I suspect, with the open corruption that seems to be aided and abetted by some of the characters in the Saigon government.

"I've heard," I said. "Who hasn't?"

"We've picked up a few enlisted men, an occasional lieutenant. But we never really have got—that is, the government hasn't got to the heart of the matter."

"I didn't know the government cared," I said with a touch of acid. "At least, I've never seen anybody from the inspector general's office prowling the black market in Saigon, or that matter looking in the funny warehouses that I recall aren't a half-dozen blocks from the presidential palace."

For the first time, Sanders looked a little defensive.

"The military has no authority to override political considerations," he said. "But that's beside the point." He was gathering the conversational reins back in his own hands. "There's been an alarming development lately, one that's got top priority." His voice dropped an impressive octave. "Marijuana."

I don't know whether he expected me to break out into a sweat. I didn't. If all the college students in the continental United States are majoring in pot, why is it such a surprise that the habit has spread to the troops? Pot had begun to appear in the service units at certain Air Force bases, I had heard, but so long as it didn't include the people who were flying the birds, it didn't make a hell of a lot of difference. Most of the pilot types had taken a cut at it on leave, but on regular missions, most of them were too scared to do anything that would dampen their reflexes.

"So some of the Joes smoke marijuana. Is that worse than three Martinis?" I asked.

Sanders looked like I had suggested I'd take Navy over Army in the annual classic and give him fourteen points to boot.

"It's the kind of practice that can corrupt our fighting men, weaken their morale and destroy their skills," he said pompously.

"Crap!" I said.

"I beg your pardon, Major," he began indignantly.

"Crap!" I repeated. "What's corrupting our fighting men is war, hopeless idiotic war that we won't win—stupid political war that buys time with the blood of some of the bravest fighting men in the history of the fighting forces."

He fooled me; I thought he was going to explode, but he merely looked at me with widened eyes and said: "You may have a point, Major."

Jacobs covered for him. "To get to the point, McKendrick, the computer indicates that the smuggling has reached into the scores of millions of dollars. Where you come in is simple: We have some evidence to believe that the proceeds of the smuggling is coming into the United States in the form of jewels, precious jewels. They're a lot more transportable than money—easier to handle, easier to hide.

"Much more important, there's additional profit in it. With inflation, there's a worldwide boom in tangibles; that's why there's been a 150 per cent increase in the value of precious stones over the last couple of years. To give you an idea, that ring of yours—"

"That alleged ring of mine," I said.

"That alleged ring of yours carries an 8 per cent duty. Smuggled in, it's worth $35,000. Hold it for a year and it's worth fifty grand, which is a nice profit for anybody."

For the first time, their suspicion began to make some

39

sense. I knew they weren't right, but it was going to be a hell of a job to prove it.

"Take a look at it from our viewpoint," urged Jacobs. "You've just come back from the Far East, where you had access to jewels like the one on the desk. Your wife has had a good deal of experience, two years, I think the record says, of buying jewelry for an Air Force boutique. In short, lots of contacts in the Far East."

I shook my head.

"You're wrong, Mr. Jacobs. Anne did none of the buying. What she did was hand the money over to the boys in the squadron, who were making flights to Singapore, Hong Kong, Thailand and so on—" I stopped suddenly because I realized where I was leading.

"That's right, Major," Jacobs said quietly. "If your wife is part of the conspiracy, she had a perfect courier organization—an Air Force squadron that flew all over the Far East, a plentiful supply of American dollars, and the perfect cover—a boutique that was actually on an American Air Force base, set up with the approval of the commanding officer. By the way, Major, it was you, was it not, who actually signed the order approving of the opening of the jewelry shop at the base?"

He had done his homework. I had talked to Pinky Prentice, our CO in Kyoto, about the boutique idea. In fact, Jane, his wife, had been one of the gals on the base who had sparked the idea. But I had signed the order as assistant CO when Pinky took off with a group of junketing congressmen for a tour of the hot spots in the capitals of our gallant allies.

"It makes a pretty picture, Mr. Jacobs," I said after a minute's thought. "There is one thing wrong with it, though."

"What's that?" He sounded interested.

"I never had $33,000 in my life. I'm a career Air Force officer. All I've got in the world is my monthly paycheck."

"I didn't say you did have $33,000, Major. All I said was somebody did have $33,000, gave it to you and you brought or sent the ring in. Or your wife did. Would you like to tell us who that person or persons are?"

I looked at the four faces around me. I couldn't see a smitch of sympathy. It dawned on me then. The crazy sons-ofbitches really did think that Anne and I had been part of a smuggling ring. I would have laughed at the thought of Anne being a tight-lipped conspirator in anything. She can't even conceal from me that she's overdrawn on our checking account.

"How do you account for her disappearance, then?" I asked. "I'm sure you've found some way to tie this in with the smuggling operation."

Logan shrugged. "You saw your house, Major. There was no sign of struggle. Obviously your wife went willingly with whoever showed up. There are a couple of possibilities. Maybe someone tipped her off to our investigation; maybe she was holding out on the smuggling group: the ring in her possession makes it look like that. You take your pick."

Again I let my eyes run from one face to the other. "I don't suppose," I said, "that it would do any good if I assured you I'm innocent of any crime and I'd stake my life on it that Anne is innocent too?"

"It would not," Sanders said coldly. "What would be more convincing would be your cooperation. If we got that, we might begin to believe in your innocence."

"What would you consider cooperation?" I asked.

"We'll suppose for the moment that you are innocent," said Sanders. "What we want you to do is sit tight, say nothing, do nothing about the kidnaping of your wife and children, if it is that. This is the first break we've had in this case and we don't want anybody to louse it up."

I looked at him with loathing. I couldn't believe that he'd said it.

"You can't mean that, Colonel," I said. "My wife and kids are gone. If you're right, if for some reason she's in the hands of the kind of people you're talking about, they'll kill her as quick as you can say Mao Tse-tung."

"You're being an alarmist, Major," said Logan. "Look at

it this way. I told you there's no point in asking for ransom if the relatives of the victim don't have it. You know, and we know, you couldn't get up a thousand dollars. So there's something else they want. There's something you have—or can get, they want. All you have to do is sit tight. As soon as they contact you, let us know. As a matter of fact, you don't even have to do that. We'll have a tap on your phone by the time you get there."

"Why should I cooperate on that basis?" I asked.

"What choice do you have?" Logan said with a shrug. "You're a career officer. If you don't cooperate, what chance do you think you have in the Air Force? You can go to the newspapers with your beef. The newspapers won't take your word for it. They'll check with our local bureau. We'll tell them that you're just back from a tough tour in Vietnam—that you've got a touch of battle fatigue and you're not really responsible for what you're saying. I think Colonel Sanders will back us up on that. Since you're by way of being a genuine hero, the newspapers will be sympathetic to our request to ignore you, for your own sake."

The kind of hate that really eats your guts out is the kind you can't do anything about. They had me by the short hairs. They knew it. I knew it. I am an Air Force officer, a damn good one, maybe one of the best, if you can measure that. It's all I know—all I want to know. I've been in twelve years. I know in my bones that the country needs people like me and Pinky Prentice and a half a thousand like them—skilled artisans at their trade, which isn't killing like the editorials say, but maintaining a level of competence behind which Congress can dawdle, the hippies can demonstrate, the citizens can complain, but they can all sleep at night. Sanders could send that dozen years of grinding work down the drain with a stroke of the pen, a curl of the lip. He didn't have to do much and I'd be out of the Air Force, and they'd make for damn sure that no airline in the country would touch me with an eleven-foot pole.

"You bastards," I said. Nobody said a word. I got to my feet slowly. "I suppose it's all right if I go home now?"

Sanders nodded permission. I looked at the ring on the desk, its green jewel winking in the harsh fluorescent light. I had a sudden thought and reached over and picked it up, started to flip it up and down in my palm.

"I don't suppose you'll tell me how you knew this was in the house," I said.

Logan shook his head.

I persisted. "When you picked it up, what did Anne say?"

He flushed a little and tightened his lips.

I've done my share of interrogating, so I knew the signs of the man who's got something to hide.

"You didn't see Anne at all, did you, Logan?"

He just looked at me silently. My mind leaped ahead to the obvious conclusion.

"Then you didn't have a warrant to enter the house? You took an anonymous tip and entered the house illegally, didn't you?"

Sanders reached for the ring and I pulled my hand away.

"You're just talking about trivialities," he said. "How we got the ring isn't important; the important thing is that we have got it."

I had no plan. I just wanted to make the bastards squirm a little. So with an appearance of total calm, I took the ring, looked at it and put it in my pocket.

"It's not quite so trivial, Colonel. The fact of the matter is that by its own admission, the FBI has been engaged in illegal search and seizure. It entered a house without a warrant, seized or stole private property. Maybe I can't sell the local papers on running the kidnaping story. But a simple-distance call to a New York or Washington newspaper is going to get them a lot of headlines. I have the feeling that with the image of J. Edgar Hoover these days, the story's going to provide a field day for the enemies of the FBI."

Logan's neck was red.

"You're being a fool, McKendrick," he said. "This won't do you any good."

Maybe it was a cheap triumph, but it was the only one I

was likely to have the whole meeting.

"To quote you my crew chief again, Logan, 'Screw you.'"

I turned to Sanders. "Now, if it's all right with you, Colonel, I'd like to be delivered to my house."

There was no mistaking the threat in his voice. "You'll cooperate?"

I looked at him for a moment in silence.

"Colonel," I said, "you make me want to vomit. I think you'd make any decent American want to vomit. Have it your way—and we throw out the old principle that a man is innocent until proven guilty. Go ahead. Use your muscle to try to keep me from finding out what happened to my family. Cooperate, sure, I'll cooperate, if I think it's good for me, for my family. But if I don't think it's good for me, you can bet your ass I'll do what I want."

"Major, it's duty to the government," he said.

I jerked my thumb at Kennedy, Jacobs and Logan.

"This is the government?" I laughed aloud and forced myself to bray like a jackass till I had walked out the door.

# 5

The corporal driving the jeep was a spit and polish type. He threw me a salute, waited till I got in, and said: "Eighty-four-oh-nine Payson Drive, right, sir?"

"Right. It's across the causeway—" I started.

"I know the section, thank you, sir," he said. He drove in silence and it was just as well. Sanders had given me more than enough to think about.

It shaped up to a nice tight box. They'd bust me out of the Air Force, without the slightest bit of compunction. High-sounding motives aside, that left me with three kids and a wife and no job, with the most obvious prospects— anything in flying—eliminated.

Despite my brave talk, I hadn't the slightest idea where

to start finding Anne and the kids, even if they'd let me. Even if I did have an idea, my total assets consisted of forty bucks in my wallet. I was pretty sure Anne had bent the checking account as far as it could go. We had only a heap of a car, and no friends with any money.

Maybe they were right, I brooded. Maybe I should sit tight, do nothing, no matter how agonizing that would be. I thought of Anne; she's not much bigger than a minute, with startling strawberry pink hair (real), a placid disposition (faked) and an affection for me and the kids (unbelievable) that makes the house a wild and loving happening every day of the year. The kids are nothing special in looks, red-haired like Anne, healthy, mischievous, as wild in their way as she is, every bit as loving. They're nothing special, unless like me you think the Cellini cup in the Metropolitan or the Mona Lisa in the Louvre are special. I'm supposed to be a pro in the business of risks;—risk-to-benefit ratio they call it in Air Intelligence. I'm supposed to know how to estimate firepower, air intelligence, terrain and all the other trade language of the fighter pilot.

But I had no kind of experience in this kind of risk estimation. I thought back there at Min Da that I'd learned something about the ultimate risks—my life and that of the squadron—but I had no experience with anything like this. At Min Da the thing on the line was our lives, but I could balance that risk against my skill and the skill of the other pilots. This risk was different. It was a different ball game—waiting for someone else to take the initiative, waiting in a game where my skills counted for nothing.

I knew I was innocent. I knew what I had paid for the ring. Seventy-three sixteen from the little Cambodian grandfather with a wisp of whisker on his otherwise smooth face. I even knew that at seventy-three sixteen he was screwing me. Anne could have gotten the ring for half that. But when I bought the ring, there was something about the thought of that tiny red head, five thousand miles and a year away, that turned me into the last of the big spenders. I remembered sending Anne the receipt. I could even see in my mind's eye the way Ying Po, the jeweler, had carefully spelled out the Cambodian riels into American dollars (in parentheses with careful brushstrokes).

I knew that all the talk about Anne using the Kyoto boutique as a cover for smugglers was unadulterated nonsense. But the ring was giving me an uncomfortable burning hole in my pocket. How did she get a $33,000 ring? Could Ying Po have made a mistake, making me the greatest bargain buyer since the Louisiana purchase? The idea was laughable.

Could he have fobbed the $33,000 ring off on me, knowing that it was going home. But how did he know that I was going to his shop? If he was part of the smuggling ring and was using me for cover, he had to be the greatest improvisor in history, sure that I'd find his shop, that he could sell me the ring, that he could persuade me to post the ring home. I struck out at the last thought. He didn't have to post the ring himself. I'd given him my home address, yes, along with my name only when he made out the bill to serve as a declaration in Customs.

I had to be honest about it. I'm like any husband in a jewelry store. I wouldn't know a piece of costume jewelry from the real thing. I pursued the thought. It would be possible to send the ring to Anne, via my ignorant hands, and later recover the ring with a simple innocent robbery that would attract no attention. I discarded that thought as quickly as it came. If there was a smuggling ring and if they did want to get jewels into the country duty-free by faking the bill of sale, I just couldn't see how they could set up a rash of robberies all over the country. Too many things could go wrong in a crime to take that kind of chance. But if Anne didn't know the ring was worth a fortune, why had she hidden the ring in her lingerie? I thought I knew—it was her specially kooky sense of intimacy, but how to explain that?

Come to that, who was the anonymous tipster who knew so much about the McKendrick home that he could tell Logan and his crowd where to put their hands on the emerald? And I was struck with another thought. What the hell was I going to do with a $33,000 ring in a home where you could open the front or back doors with a hair pin? And a lot of strange people seemed to be doing just that.

I felt like a harried rabbit: I was doing a lot of running, but I couldn't find a hole to hide in.

My backside told me the jeep was braking for Maplewood Avenue and the corporal turned left.

"It's right, Corporal, not left," I said automatically.

"Very good, sir," he said. "It's a dead-end street. I'll make a turn there. Sorry about that."

The beam of the headlights picked up the "Dead End" sign on the white fence and he turned skillfully into a driveway, alongside a large dark house. It took him no more than ten seconds and if he was being observed, it would have looked like he was doing no more than looking behind for directions.

"Wait twenty minutes after you get in the house, Major," he said in a clipped voice. "Leave the lights on, slip out the back door and go through the back lot. Go one street right and four left. You'll see a sign on a late-hours grocery: 'Hernandez.' Go to the back door, knock twice and go on in."

I looked sharply at him. I had heard the words, but I really didn't take it in.

"One right, four left, Hernandez' grocery store," I repeated.

He didn't say another word till he dropped me in front of the house. Then he said in a loud voice: "Good night, sir." In a low tone, one I could barely hear over the clash of the gears, he added: "Regards from Sergeant Halloran."

I watched the jeep take off and its taillights disappearing around the corner. Just as he turned the corner I saw a car turn into the street; then it headed into one of the farthest driveways. I pretended not to notice that it didn't pull far enough into the driveway to approach the garage. Instead I walked up the flagstone walk and let myself into the house.

I turned on most of the lights, flipped on the television set. I wanted to be certain that if anyone approached the door, they'd hear it. I stepped up the volume and hoped

47

that my neighbors, the Friendlys, wouldn't be disturbed. I got a glass of milk and a couple of cookies, put on the lights in the hallways, the bedroom lights upstairs and then doused the downstairs light.

I slipped out onto the back porch and moved into the shadows. I knew I had another ten minutes to wait before I could move out, but I thought I had a better chance of escaping notice if I hid in the darkness. A little too late I noticed that I was still in the light sports jacket I'd put on when I headed for the Officers' Club, and I wished I'd had the brains to change to something more inconspicuous.

I looked at my watch. It was ten twenty and I felt a feeling of relief. Unless they'd changed the practice at the base, one of the shifts went off at ten o'clock. Unless they'd changed the street since I'd been overseas, the percentage was that eight out of the ten families on the street were MacDill personnel. It was a good bet that one of them was on the ten-o'clock shift. That would bring him home at approximately ten thirty. I'd wait. If I got the expected break, I could slip out under the cover of the car turning into my street. The headlights would momentarily blind whoever might be watching, unless all my training in night flying were wrong. We figured over Nam that a flash of light obtruding on a darkened cabin gave you virtual blindness for approximately eight seconds.

I heard the car coming, saw the sudden flash of its lights, ducked off the porch and started running lightly on the balls of my feet alongside my garage. I made only one mistake and it saved my life. I was going hell-bent alongside the garage when without warning I hit something hard with my right leg and went ass over teakettle onto the ground. Even as I was falling, I heard the thud on the side of the garage, a moment of silence and then the echo of footsteps pounding away from the garage. Skinned knees and all, I sprang to my feet, ready to follow. Then I had a second thought. It was dark out there. Whoever it was, he had a solid advantage over me. I put out my hand and leaned on the side of the garage. I remembered the thud and I started feeling along the wall. I found it when I felt the pain in my hand. I couldn't light a match, but by scrooging around, I could see it in the fragrant wisps of moonlight that seeped through the palmettos. It was a knife, about eight inches long, but only seven inches were showing. The knife was buried more than an inch in the wall.

Suddenly, the sweat under my arms turned icy cold, as I realized if I hadn't fallen over whatever it was alongside the garage, the knife would have been buried in my chest and a hell of a lot deeper than that inch in the pine clapboard. I got down on my hands and knees and felt around with my fingers to find out what I tripped over. It was the garden rake and I thanked God that all the lectures, all the whacks on the fanny hadn't yet trained Shane to put things away in their proper places.

On suddenly weakened knees, I pulled myself to my feet and tugged the knife from the garage wall. It came out hard. In the movies, the hero sticks spare knives in his belt, but I couldn't see how I could do that without slashing my abdomen. I settled for tearing off the tail of my shirt, wrapping it around the blade and tucking the knife in my inside jacket pocket.

I started to move out to my rendevous at Hernandez' and suddenly stopped dead still. The only one who knew —really knew that I was going out the garage way was Halloran. With that came a feeling of nausea. I hadn't realized till now how I had been depending on Halloran and it looked like he'd set me up for the kill. Why, I didn't know, but he fitted, he fitted like a glove. He had total access to MacDill, and while I don't know the exact number, I knew that scores of planes, maybe as many as a hundred, went through there every day from all over the world. One more thing: it's currently the major takeoff point for pilots headed for the Vietnam theater. It would be no trick at all for Halloran to serve as central contact man for pilots going in or out—to pick up merchandise from them, to pass along directions.

Halloran knew my house, too. He'd been there only

three, four, maybe half a dozen times, but enough for a man skilled in observation. Supposing something had gone wrong at the Cambodian end—that I'd wound up with the emerald ring instead of another American pilot. Supposing Halloran got the job of picking it up and muffed the job. What better way of shutting off one phase of the operation than getting rid of me? I took a deep breath, reached into my jacket pocket and took the knife out. I stripped the rag, carefully stowed the blade up my sleeve and tightened my fingers around the shaft. I had the feeling Halloran was like all of us in the military. We're accustomed to weapons powerful enough to blow a whole platoon to bits. But none of us have got the stomach for the naked blade up against the belly or the throat.

I had to go slowly. I still didn't know whether my unknown assailant was out in front of me. I coppered my bet. I cut through the backyard lots for five streets, not the one suggested by the corporal. That way I came on the Hernandez grocery store from the wrong side. The section is like a lot of semighetto areas in Tampa, and Hernandez' is like a half a hundred Ma and Pa stores with pink bananas, plantains and other decaying produce in the window, and with dusty half-filled shelves lit up by a couple of bare bulbs. I could see an old woman, moving around slowly, giving a lazy swipe at the shelves with an ancient feather duster. Her heart wasn't in it. I slipped around the back, found the door and listened. I couldn't hear a sound.

You get a delicate touch when you fly an F-4; you better or you're dead. I turned the knob with my left hand as carefully as if I were making a 4-G bank. I had the naked blade pointing ahead of me, with the point slightly tilted up, like a wary sergeant in the infantry had told me you should. I flung the door open, slammed into the room and had the knife at the side of Halloran's jugular vein before he had a chance to turn around.

"Easy, boy," I told him tensely, "or I cut myself a piece of throat."

He didn't move a muscle. His hand stayed on the bottle

of Three Vines, and the other hung on to the fat Cuban cigar.

"Don't 'boy' me, Major," he said calmly, "unless you really intend to use that knife. I long ago got over taking that kind of crap, even from gold-plated majors."

For answer, I increased the pressure of the blade's edge the tiniest bit. He was a tough one—the cigar held steady as a rock—but a tiny bead of perspiration started to well and slide down his temple.

"Why'd you set me up, Halloran?" I asked harshly. "Who's your knife-throwing friend?"

"I don't know what's eating on your tail, Major," he said, "but you already got big trouble. Cutting my throat ain't going to bring you back that pretty little wife and those nice kids. If you take a minute to think about it, you got to remember one thing. I'm the only hope you got. I already got my ass in a sling once for you, and like an idiot, I'm coming back for more."

I had no choice. I tossed the knife on the table in front of him and moved around to face him.

"A very sensible decision," said a crisp voice behind me. Startled, I turned around. The man in the doorway had the gun pointed squarely at my middle. How long he had been there I didn't know, but there was no mistaking the determination in the narrowed eyes, the tight-lipped mouth in the handsome Latin face. Being the target for people with lethal weapons twice in one night was a little bit too much. I dropped weakly into a chair at the table.

"Whoooo!" said Halloran, expelling a great gust of breath. "I haven't been that scared since I was sixteen on the South Side of Philadelphia."

He pushed a glass across the table and poured out a healthy slug of brandy. He looked over his shoulder. "You'll join us, Captain?"

The slim man holstered the gun and moved closer to the table. "In a moment, thank you, Sergeant. Let's get the Major's story first." He sat on the edge of the table. "I don't look favorably on knives in my town, Major. I'd like an explanation—quick and complete—or you'll find out what the tank in Tampa is like."

He laid his identification on the table: "Captain Julio Hernandez, Tampa Police." He picked up the knife, ran a thumbnail along the blade, hefted it in his right hand.

I told it from the beginning—the corporal's message, the precise directions to the grocery store, the thrown knife, my luck in stumbling, and I finished: "You add it up, Captain. The only one who knew I was coming, when and by what route, was Halloran."

He shook his head. "That is not precisely true, Major. Two other persons at least knew all those things—the corporal and myself."

I was startled. Hernandez nodded. "Yes, Major, I set up this meeting, not Sergeant Halloran. I can give you my personal assurances that I have no wish to see you dead. On the contrary, I wish you very much alive."

"The corporal, Sergeant—is he trustworthy?"

Halloran loosed his tie, opened three buttons on his blouse. The undershirt was startlingly white against his black skin. He pulled the shirt up, stood so the light shone on his abdomen. The eight-inch scar from chest down below his pants line was like the angry puckered mouth of an animal.

"I got that at Chosun Reservoir. McCallum—Corporal McCallum—carried me eleven miles on his back to get me home alive. That enough for you?"

Hernandez nodded. "That leaves my office," he said thoughtfully. Halloran looked at him wide-eyed.

"Your office?"

Hernandez looked at him sadly. "It could very well be; it won't be the first time. Indeed it is not so surprising. My phone call to you, Sergeant, was made from the detective's common room." He looked over at me. "The Tampa police force does not enjoy the most commodious of quarters, Major. My own office was being used for an interrogation and I used a phone in an open area. I had no reason to think I was being overheard. Apparently I was, and I apologize for the inconvenience caused you."

Halloran grinned. "You do have a way with words, Captain, I do declare. Inconvenience, hah! How about a drink?"

"Please." Hernandez sniffed at the liquor delicately, then took a dainty sip.

"Major," he said to me, "if you can overlook my carelessness which endangered your life, I should like you to tell me what happened at the base tonight. Perhaps I can be of assistance in your problem."

Halloran refilled my glass. I told them the whole story, from Kennedy's original visit down to my jeep ride home. Hernandez listened intently, his head tipped a bit in my direction.

"You have the ring with you?" he asked. I handed it to him and he examined it carefully in the light.

"It is Colonel Sanders' belief then that this is a genuine Colombian emerald, purchased in Cambodia, and it has a value of approximately $33,000?"

"Yes," I said.

He bobbed his head in satisfaction. "I would have enjoyed being there when you walked out with this. I do not think Colonel Sanders is accustomed to opposition to his wishes."

"Can you find Anne and my children?" I asked abruptly.

"I shall be perfectly frank with you, Major," he said soberly. "It has been made abundantly clear to me that I am to keep hands off the matter of your wife and children."

"Logan?"

"Yes."

"What can they threaten you with? Can they demote you and put you to walking a beat in the suburbs?" The bitterness came through in my voice.

"Major McKendrick, for what I am about to say I must apologize in advance. I do this because I have been told by Sergeant Halloran that you are a good man, an understanding one. So please listen.

"I am the highest-ranking officer on the Tampa police force with a Cuban background. The Cubans are quite

53

close to a majority in the town. I need not tell you that they have had a harder time with the local police force than perhaps their normally extroverted actions require. It has taken me nearly twenty years to arrive in my present position. It has not been easily arrived at—and it can be lost in the blinking of a city official's eye.

"I have done a good job for my people, Major, in two ways." He held up an elegant hand and ticked off his points. "First, in the words of Halloran's people, I have taught them to 'cool it,' and second, in my own advance, I have helped to sell them on the idea that the whole police force is not made up of white, club-swinging, head-breaking Florida crackers. My people are important to me and ordinarily—" he underscored the word—"I would not jeopardize that by sticking my nose in a case where the FBI has warned me off it. Mr. Hoover can get very active on the telephone to prominent politicians who admire his brand of law and order."

I've been at too many southern Air Force bases not to know precisely the kind of reverse grapevine that could make the life of Captain Hernandez very uncomfortable indeed. I nodded my agreement.

He held his glass out to Halloran.

"*Gracias, mi amigo,*" he said politely, and sipped delicately again. "But," he said harshly, "the rules of the game have been changed, Major McKendrick. A cop has been killed—an unimportant little man, Frank Martinez."

He shook his head at my unspoken question.

"No, it is not that he is of Cuban descent. He was a cop and it is not practical for the murder of a policeman, black, white or brown, to go unpunished, regardless of the combined wishes of Mr. J. Edgar Hoover, Mr. Logan and those of your Colonel Sanders. I shall move carefully—very carefully indeed, Major, but I shall move."

He looked broodingly at the knife.

"Do you know what this is—its type, its origin, Major McKendrick?"

"No, I am sorry. I do not."

"It is, I think, Russian. We have discovered identical types when we have been fortunate enough to make a successful raid on Fidelista hideouts. It is our belief that they have been provided by the Russians to certain revolutionary training centers. Curiously enough, the knife took its form from a superb knife provided during World War II to certain SS troops. The Germans love knives, almost as much as the Cubans—the Latins," he amended. "They too value it as a sign of *machismo*."

I reached out for the knife, examined it under the light, took it between my fingertips and weighed it for balance.

"No, not that way," he said, taking the knife gently from my fingers. "Like so." He laid it gently in the palm of his hand, the blade pointing away from the fingertips. The arm moved like the flick of a snake's tongue and I heard the knife thud into the door. I turned my head; the knife was quivering under the naked breast of a remarkably handsome dark girl on a calendar, advertising the navy beans of Montoya y Cia.

Halloran got out of his chair, retrieved the knife. "Papa Hernandez isn't going to like his pinup ruined."

The police captain smiled. "He has others, more brazen, in the drawer. That is merely a cover to distract Aunt Viola."

He held his hand out for the knife. There was a diamond-hard glitter to his brown-black eyes.

"I took a knife, precisely like this one, from the chest of Frank Martinez last night, in a warehouse at the foot of Bougainvillea Street. I also took this from a spot only a few feet from his body. We think it was dropped in a struggle with his murderer."

He took a bit of white tissue paper from his wallet, opened it carefully and put it on the table alongside Anne's ring. Even to the unpracticed eye, the cold green glitter was identical.

Halloran asked the question for me.

"Colombian?"

"Colombian," said Hernandez.

# 6

Maybe it's a bad habit, but when you put your hide on the line like I'd been doing for the past thirteen months, you don't believe everything they tell you in the briefing session. They have a tendency to smooth over the rough spots, to leave out the significant detail. The first couple of times you get a tailful of tracers up your backside, you tend to get angry.

And later on you get the picture. The guy with the well-pressed pants and the microphone and the pointer, with a smooth-looking sergeant to handle the maps, has got his job. His job is to get the thing done.

It's a little scary the first couple of times, because you sit there and realize he's counting the house like the manager of a struggling play on Broadway. He's saying to himself: "Yes sir, general, sir. We've got 120 of them out there. The law of averages says 102 of them will get back with minimum damage. Of the 18, 11 will get the whole package. Of the 11 pilots, the Jolly Green Giants will be able to pick up 4 in the helicopters. Of the other 7, they'll go on the list as 'missing in action'—who knows what the hell that means, these days? The remaining 7 birds will suffer 'severe damage.' That means 1 will crash-land, 2 will make it to nearby bases, 4 will make it, but plane or pilot will suffer damage to make him or it as the case may be inoperable."

But what the natives will tell you on Long Island Sound and the Chesapeake and the shorelines of Louisiana is that after they've heard the shotguns the first couple of times, the ducks get smarter. They get leery of the suspicious spots, the quiet areas, the well-grained bits of water. And when you've had a solid piece of the Vietnam bit, you begin to read the telltale omissions in the briefings. You better learn to read them, otherwise you get dead in a hurry.

To give you a for instance, when the man with the microphone tells you: "Intelligence has no specific information on this sector, but the best information would indicate that it is lightly defended," watch that one, Jack! What he's really saying is: "We lost a bird here the other day. Can't imagine why. Must be they got something new in here."

Or the other one, they wind up almost every briefing with: "Every effort must be made to destroy the military objective, but total vigilance must be observed by the pilot and navigator to avoid unnecessary civilian harassment." That means, "Screw it, hit anything that moves." If the fellow from the boss man says: "Every effort must be made to destroy the military objective, and only the military objective," that means: "For Christ's sake, fellows, hold up the rockets and the napalm; headquarters has got word there are a couple of nosy correspondents in the area."

I've taken so long to get through this because I had the distinct feeling I was getting a high-level briefing from Captain Hernandez. He was giving me, for a fact, the military objective, but only the highlights of the difficulties. In short, I was getting the message that like the two-star general, sitting alongside the computer in Saigon, muttering to himself: "They can't do that to *my* Air Force," Hernandez was grinding an ax all his own. I know he wanted to help get Anne and the kids back, and for all I could tell, he even thought I was innocent of jewel thievery, smuggling, etc. But I also had the feeling he was being awfully Latin and devious.

I put the question carefully. "You figure then, Captain Hernandez, that my problem and the murder of Frank Martinez are linked. We've got the knives, we've got the emeralds. You deduce from the knives that because of the Russian origin, somehow, somewhere, this is mixed up with the Fidelistas and specifically with these Fidelistas being trained for revolutionary activity in Latin and South America, trained in some place or places unknown?"

"Guatemala," he said politely. "The most recent reports pinpoint Guatemala."

"Information courtesy the FBI or the CIA?" I asked.

"Neither," he said. "They take; they don't give."

From the expression on his face, it was an open sore.

"You have a line on the man who killed Martinez?"

"Nothing definite," he said evasively.

"What indefinite?" I challenged.

Hate blazed through his eyes. They looked totally black to me then.

"Among the factors reported by the coroner on the body of Frank Martinez as significant was the fact that the fingers of both hands had been crushed. It was the opinion of the coroner that the injuries were inflicted after death. They have all the earmarks of having been inflicted by the heels of boots. Similar injuries were found twice in the last three years on murder victims. We canvassed various police forces, asking for information on similar injuries to murder victims. The Mexico City police reported two similar cases. They believe the injuries and the murders were committed by a Cuban of uncertain age and description known only as El Rojo."

It seemed unlikely, but I had to ask the question. "You mean, he's a redheaded Cuban?"

"It is not thought so, Major," Hernandez said coldly. "The Mexico City police felt it more likely El Rojo, The Red, referred to the blood that accompanied his murders. So it was also thought along the waterfront, where he was last reputed to have been seen."

"What do you want of me?" I asked bluntly.

His eyes widened a trifle and he muttered something rapidly in Spanish. Halloran grinned and translated: "The man who lives with danger treads carefully on the steps of his homestead." He asked the captain: "Cervantes?"

"Hernandez." The policeman smiled.

He had a speculative look in his eyes. It's the same look you find in the eyes of the boys who've been in command for some time. How much shall I tell them? the look says.

"Excuse me," he said suddenly, and went through the door on which the punctured pinup was hanging.

Halloran looked at me quizzically.

"How far can I trust him?" I asked.

He opened his huge hands, palms up and shrugged. "You got a choice, Major baby? I'll give you this: He's straight as a string. Only one thing: He gets his mind set on something, there ain't much give in him."

"Can he help me get my wife and kids back?"

"Somebody's got to," Halloran said simply. "The way I look at it, you got three government bureaus know about your wife and kids—the FBI, the Air Force and the inspector general's office. They got all the muscle any ordinary citizen needs to find his wife and kids. But they're not using that muscle for you. They're just leaning on you to do one thing—sit still. I hate to say it, Major, but they got you in their plans for just one thing. You're the judas-goat, staked out in one spot, till the leopard moves. I also got a very peculiar feeling they don't really give much of a damn if you get all bloodied—or even if your wife and kids get all bloodied, so long as they catch themselves a leopard. Could be, too, if the leopard don't get caught moving in on you, they got themselves another lamb somewhere or they'll get one."

He didn't have the answer, of course, but I had to put the question in words.

"Christ, Sergeant, they can't do that to me, can they? The government, I mean. They can't use me, my wife and my kids in some kind of cops-and-robbers game. Even if there is the kind of smuggling they talk about, how can you match a girl and three kids against money? Jesus, don't they owe me something for the last twelve years?"

He took a couple of deep drags on his cigar and puffed them out in great fat clouds. He took a leisurely drink from his brandy glass.

"How old are you, Major?" he asked.

"What the hell has that to do with it? Thirty-four, if it makes any difference."

"Thirty-four. Whooee. It's awful late to be learning, Major. Now me, Major, I learned that at my Moma's knee when I wasn't ass high to a chamberpot. The Man—The Man, Major—he do what he think right and he don't want no back talk from the like of little folks, specially little folks that happen to be black. Now you don't remember Charley Johnson. He put in for retirement a year ago after twenty-two years. I told him he was out of his mind to go back to Dallas County, but he'd always liked it around Selma, where he spent a couple of hitches. He went, him and his wife, a nice girl named Mabel. Got a note from Mabel the other day, enclosing a newspaper clipping. The clipping didn't say much. Just said: Charles Johnson, a resident of Pomeroy, died suddenly on Tuesday, last week. He was an Air Force veteran."

He took his cigar out of his mouth and squinted along its length like he was sighting down a rifle barrel.

"You know what it means in an Alabama newspaper, a county seat newspaper when it says a Negro 'died suddenly,' Major? It means he was lynched. Come to find out, Charley got himself mixed up with a voting registration thing. He figured he'd given twenty-two years to the government and he was entitled to ask. Like I said before, Major, The Man, he do what he thinks is right for him and he don't want no back talk from no little folks, black or white. Black *or* white, Major."

He poured a dollop of brandy in my glass.

"Drink up, Major. It could be a long night."

I drank it slowly. It tasted bitter.

He smiled at me. "One thing, Major, you could figure on for what it's worth."

"What's that?" I said dully.

"Strange thing. There a bit of Charley Johnson in all of us. I've been sitting here figuring and I made up my mind. I'd kind of like to take a crack at The Man myself. Don't matter a dog's dinner to me whether it's the FBI, the Air Force, the inspector general or even the sovereign state of Georgia. Whatever you're getting into, and for whatever comfort it is to you, you could figure that Bradford Sherman Halloran is right there beside you."

The sudden glow I felt didn't just come from the brandy. "You could get busted from the Air Force."

"I put in twenty-seven years," he said. "They can't take that from me, no matter what."

He started to chuckle.

"Ain't that a hell of a middle name for a black boy born in Valdosta, Georgia, Major? Sherman, by God! My old man, he sure had a peculiar sense of humor."

The door opened and Hernandez came in carrying a tray. On the tray was an old-fashioned coffee percolator, a couple of thick cups and a bowl of lump sugar. He filled a cup for each of us, put a lump of sugar on his spoon and carefully poured the brandy till the lump was thoroughly soaked, then stirred it slowly into the thick black liquid. We followed his example. I tasted the coffee. It was strong for my taste, but it had a marvelous cleansing effect on my mouth.

"Excellent coffee, Captain," I said politely.

"My aunt will be pleased," he said. "I have a suggestion, Major, that I would like to expose for your consideration."

Out of the corner of my eye, I saw Halloran sit up alertly. I took a long gulp of coffee to clear my head. I'd listen to Hernandez, but I wanted to listen awfully slow. I wasn't sure that I wanted to trust him all that much.

"I'd like to hear it."

He crossed his knees, sat back in his chair and balanced his cup delicately on his knee. I was reminded of the professional ease of the briefing officer at Ubon.

"As one sees this situation, Major, it is clear that the people on the other side, presumably those who have your wife and children, are expecting you to sit dead still until they contact you. So, too, are your Air Force and its co-operating government agencies. In short, both groups believe they can benefit from your inaction.

"I have considered the matter carefully from your standpoint. I see no advantage from your standpoint in inaction. Your objective is clear. You want your wife and children back. Yet the Air Force and the FBI, clearly with all the tools on their side, are making no effort to aid you in your search.

61

"If you cooperate with your unknown enemies, they will presumably pledge the return of your family. I regret to say that the statistics on the return of kidnap victims do not favorably impress me. I should say under the circumstances outlined, the probability is that you will not see your wife and children alive again."

I heard the calm voice with growing horror. He had surgically sliced the veil in my subconscious where I had buried that dreadful thought.

"I'm afraid you must accept the idea, Major," he said gently. "Kidnapers do not like witnesses."

He waited till I was able to talk. "Yes, Major?"

"What are you suggesting, Captain Hernandez?" I asked harshly.

"I suggest we return the initiative to our side, Major."

"How?"

"Simple," he said. "Both the government and the criminals believe that you are a pawn to be moved at their discretion. I suggest we change that."

"How?"

He reached into his pocket and pulled out Anne's ring. I had forgotten he had kept it.

"This," he said quietly. "In a way in which I am not sure, this emerald is the key to the whole matter. It is clear that both the Air Force and your enemies expect you to sit still with this in your hand, waiting for instructions."

"How can they know—the people who have Anne, I mean—how can they know I have the ring?"

"They need not know that you have it," he said. "They can be reasonably certain that you have access to it. Like you, they would find it incredible that when your family is faced with a threat of death or worse, an agency of the United States government would not surrender the jewel."

"It makes sense. So what do I do?"

"I want you to consider, Major, what would happen if the plans of both parties were disrupted—if, in fact, the jewel were not in your control."

"They'd kill Anne and the kids," I said tightly.

He shook his head. "You're not thinking, Major. They might murder your wife and children if they knew you had the ring and refused to surrender it. But if they know, know positively, you don't have the ring, I believe two things will happen. We will buy precious time for your wife and children while the kidnapers try to figure the new problem out and possibly change their plans. The most important thing we're going to do is to heave a rock into a deep and dirty pool and see where the ripples go."

I turned the idea over in my mind. It was just possible that he might be right. But his idea had something more important going for it. At least I'd be doing something.

"How can we be sure they will know I no longer have the ring?"

He held the bottle of brandy to me.

"What does it say on the label, Major?"

"*Tres Cepas,*" I read.

"Right," he said briskly, "Three Vines. We shall put the information into the grapevine. We can take it for granted that we're dealing with criminals. A criminal organization, precisely like the police organization, is only as good as its information—and information is only as good as it is fresh or current. We'll put the ring where it cannot be ignored."

Halloran said quickly: "Papa Mendoza?"

"Precisely," Hernandez said approvingly.

"Who's Mendoza?" I asked.

"The leading fence in town," said Hernandez, "an evil, wily and highly successful old man. It has been our belief that more than twenty per cent of all the stolen property in this part of the state passes through his hands."

"If he's that notorious," I asked cautiously, "how come you haven't nailed him?"

"There's an old saying in the Bible, Major, that explains it," he replied. " 'The children of mammon are wiser in their generation than the children of light.' Papa Mendoza is a professional; he's every bit as good at his job—handling stolen goods—as you are at flying an airplane. Perhaps a lot better. He's lived a lot longer at his profession than you have. If we could spend on crime generally all the hours we've spent trying to trap Papa Mendoza, I think the crime rate would be down ten per cent."

"I don't see how we're going to con a man that clever into taking on the emerald ring."

"You will forgive me, Major," said Hernandez, "but you do not know Papa Mendoza. He is an artist in his business. I said he was clever and wily. But he has the boldness of the true entrepreneur. He enjoys working under the very noses of the police department. It will not be easy to bait the trap, but it can be done with the proper intermediaries."

He eyed Sergeant Halloran. "I can have your cooperation as well?"

"*Por supuesto,*" the Negro said. "Papa and I have had a brush or two before." He looked at me. "His shop on Figueroa is the first port of call when some GI has been rolled. I must have been in his shop about fifty or sixty times inquiring if a watch has been pawned. It never has been, according to Papa."

"Good," Hernandez said decisively. "I shall make the other arrangements. It will not do for you, Major, to approach Papa directly. It must be done through channels."

I raised my eyebrows.

"As I have mentioned," he explained, "it is impossible to function without a reliable set of informers. I shall study our list of contacts for the proper person. He can inform Papa Mendoza of the availability of the emerald, of your rather desperate need for money to aid you in your search and of the somewhat suspicious nature of the ring. Sergeant Halloran will reinforce that suspicion by making Papa Mendoza aware of the official Air Force interest in the jewel. Then I shall let you know."

"That will be difficult," I said. "Have you forgotten they've bugged my phone?"

He snapped his fingers in disgust. "Of course, stupid of me. Let me think." He sought inspiration in the ceiling.

"Paco?" Halloran mentioned the name softly; there was a slight grin on his lips.

An expression of distaste crossed Hernandez' face.

"That keeps it in the family, Captain," added Halloran. Hernandez' tightened lips conveyed clearly he'd bitten into something bad.

"Yes," he said finally. "It had better be Paco."

"Who is Paco? And do we know we can trust him?" I asked.

Hernandez showed a slight air of embarrassment.

"Unfortunately, Major, he is a distant relative of mine. He is also a procurer, a pusher of narcotics, a petty thief and I suspect as well, a possible murderer. He is not to be trusted; that is precisely the point. He is so untrustworthy that he will be believed by Papa Mendoza, who probably knows more about Paco than I do. It raises however one unfortunate point."

The embarrassment had deepened—a slight tinge of red suffused the handsome *café au lait* face.

"Paco will demand a commission—one from you as well as one from Papa Mendoza. It is more than likely that even after you have made your arrangement with Papa Mendoza, Paco will try to blackmail you."

"How much can I get for the ring?" I asked.

Hernandez frowned. "You have a valuation of $33,000, you tell me, from a legitimate dealer. You ought to get around twenty-five per cent. Under the circumstances, however, with Paco in the act and with Sergeant Halloran raising certain other suspicions, you'll be lucky to get $5,000. I'm afraid you can count on paying another $1,000 to Paco. It is an expensive bit of diversion, Major."

"Will it help get Anne and the kids back, Captain?"

He shrugged, threw out his hands. "I have no other idea, Major."

"It's cheap," I said. "After all, I did pay seventy-three sixteen for it."

I saw a flicker of scepticism flash across his eyes. He covered it quickly by bringing his coffee cup to his face.

"Paco will call you after four o'clock tomorrow afternoon. The name Hernandez is so common in the area that he need

65

not use any other. You will ask him if he can get you eight pounds of *Café Beneficia,* but green beans only."

"*Café Beneficia,* green beans, eight pounds," I repeated.

"Correct, Major. It is a brand of coffee well known in the inner city but not sold in quantities such as the more common brands. It is a little hard to get hold of unless you are familiar with our more exotic *bodegas.* You will tell him that this was suggested by Sergeant Malone. Is that right, Sergeant Halloran?"

"Who's Malone?" I asked.

"Like he said about Paco," Halloran said grimly, "Malone's a part-time procurer, petty thief—you name it. I've got enough on him to get him ten years in Leavenworth and he knows it. I'll give him enough to whet Paco's appetite. The greedy little bastard will go to Mendoza."

We went over the whole thing again before Hernandez was satisfied that I knew my role. I was wearied; it seemed like I'd spent the entire last twenty-four hours in the back of the local grocery store.

Halloran got up, stuck out his hand: "I'll split now. Like they say in the movies, Don't call me, I'll call you." He grinned "I won't forget the tap."

Hernandez led me out the back door. There was a beat-up grocery panel-truck standing near the door.

"Get in the back," he said. "I'll drive you most of the way home, cut in two streets behind your house—you make your way over the back lots."

I squatted down behind the driver's seat of the panel truck. One thing had been nagging me for a long time.

"Captain?"

"Yes, Major?"

"One question: What are you going to do about the man in your department, the one who informed our enemies of your plans and set me up for the knifing?"

I saw him stiffen, then sit more erect.

"It is a matter for the police department, Major Mc-Kendrick, and no concern of yours." The voice was stilted officialese.

I look at the stiffened back. The disgust rose from deep within me and sat like an undissolved aspirin in my throat.

"You know, Captain Hernandez, I just discovered two things."

"Yes, Major, what are those?"

"Brass is brass the world over and it doesn't matter a damn what uniform it's on. You're not a goddamned bit better than Colonel Sanders. All he cares about is the reputation of the Air Force. All you're concerned with is the reputation of the local police force and getting even with the people who knifed one of your cops. Sanders wanted to stake me out like a goat as bait for the leopards. You're a bit fancier. You've cut the halter and you're shooing me right into the leopard's den. I hope you don't regret it. I hope you won't spend the rest of your life thinking how your smartass plan got my wife and kids killed."

He didn't turn his head but kept staring through the windshield.

"I hope for both our sakes, Major, that I won't."

He let the truck coast to a halt under the dense shadow of a couple of trees.

"Here we are, Major, two blocks from your house."

I get up, ready to move out.

"A moment, Major," he said. "Take this." He handed me the knife my would-be killer had left behind. "It is a hard world where Paco and Papa Mendoza make their living."

I hopped out lightly and he leaned from the car window. "*Vaya con Dios,* Major."

# 7

I had only one bad moment making my way back to the house—when I came to the side of the garage where I had almost been knifed. Try as I might, I couldn't slide through that dark patch of shadow. Instead, I chickened out, circled the other side of the garage, hurried up the back steps and let myself into the house.

I stood inside the kitchen door, breathing heavily.

All I could hear was the sound track of the TV. I went into the living room, snapped off the inevitable Randolph Scott western and slumped down on the couch.

In the sudden silence, unbroken save by the creaking of an empty house, I felt a wave of sadness break through the cocoon of disbelief that my mind had mercifully spun to keep the awful reality away.

It was no trick at all to people that room with the ones I loved best, as they were last Christmas, two days before I had taken off for Nam. It was (except when the colonel's wife came for the monthly squadron coffee)—a hell of a mess. Anne was wearing the pink stretch pants and the aquamarine blouse that were her favorite combination. With her hair, I thought it was stunning. She was shuttling between the kitchen stove and the eddy, surge and hurricane made up of three children with the Christmas presents still new enough to keep them on the happy side of hysteria.

I was lounging on the couch, with the F-4 manual open on my lap. I had lived with the goddamned manual for a year and I suppose the only reason I was reading it again on Christmas Day was some deep determination to leave nothing undone that might bring me back safely to the four of them.

It wasn't much of a Christmas as those things go. But the memory was almost enough to keep me sane during the thirteen months between then and now. It was a blur of Christmas tree lights, battery-operated toys, scattered bits of wrapping paper, Polaroid pictures, sudden wails of injury, momentary argument, the festive meal, bubble baths, and Anne falling asleep in my lap on the couch when the house had become finally and blessedly quiet.

It was literally impossible for me now to think of them in danger; I avoided the uglier words, but the blank silence in the house crowded in around me. I was exhausted, but I didn't really want to go to bed. The ringing of the door chimes startled me, so that I scrambled out of the couch. Something ripped loudly and I looked down. I had for-

68

gotten. I had slipped the knife into my hip pocket and in my anxious squirming, I had worked it loose, into the sofa upholstery beside the cushion.

The doorbell chimes rang again, and for a moment I debated taking the knife with me, concealed behind my hip. "The hell with it," I said, and shoved it down into the side of a chair out of sight.

I switched on the porch light and hated myself for the moment of hesitant wariness before I pulled the door open. The man on the porch was about my size. Like all of us, he wore the standard off-duty uniform, sports shirt and chinos. He also had a big grin on his face and a hand stuck through the door.

"Major McKendrick?" he asked. "Bill Friendly, Papa Bear of the brood that are now your next-door neighbors."

"Pleased to meet you, Captain, isn't it?" I smeared a phony heartiness over the reluctance in my voice. "Come on in." I stepped back from the door.

"No sirree, Bob," he said. "I'm a man with a mission. I came over with orders from my wife to bring you right back with me. We got a pot of coffee on the stove and there's an apple pie like you haven't tasted since Thanksgiving in New England. She said it loud and clear: 'Bring the man back and don't take no for an answer.'" He gave me a real gleaming Rotary Club set of teeth.

I was a little ashamed of myself. At other times, I would have been kind. I would have said my neighbor, Bill Friendly, was a hell of a nice guy. But in the mood I was in, he was coming on much too strong, much too "long time no see." But I couldn't refuse. Air Force developments are tiny enclaves, where a surly neighbor is more trouble than he's worth. I suppose it's a product of the kind of closed society we live in, where we share the same troubles, the same small gratifications, the same incomes, the same debts, the same irritations—a closely sheltered life, where the mere fact of difference can create resentment.

"Let me get a jacket," I said. I reached in the closet alongside the front door.

"Mrs. McKendrick in bed?" he asked. "Maybe if she's still awake, she can throw a robe on over her 'jamas and join us."

"She's not home at the moment," I said, closing the door after me.

"By golly," he said, "I do remember now. Maude told me something about you two getting your messages fouled up and missing each other. Too bad; we'd have liked to get to know her real quick."

We went, Air Force *de rigueur,* in the back door and into the kitchen. I remembered Mrs. Friendly from the brief talk we had, but her husband grabbed her round the shoulders and said: "Major McKendrick, I'd like you to meet my Mama Bear."

I saw her wince a little, rather like the way Anne winces when she hears me say yes to the third Martini. Worse was yet to come. The guy walked into the living room (the houses in the kind of development we live in are exactly alike even to the leaking showers) and brought back a photograph. They were good-looking children, but I'd bet he'd already turned them into lifetime enemies. He held out the picture and said: "And here are the three little bears."

I liked Mrs. Friendly better instantly. She said wearily: "Oh, Bill. That's so corny."

Most guys get embarrassed at something like that, but I saw a quick narrowing of his eyes, a whitening around the nose. I felt myself saying to myself: "There's a mean streak in that bastard."

He covered it up quickly. "Right, honey. Actually, Major, their names are Tom, Dick and Harry." I thought he was having me on, but those were the kids' names. I found myself overpraising their looks, with bleak thoughts of my own three in my mind.

One thing Friendly wasn't kidding about was the pie: it was delicious. I wound up a half-hour later taking home half of it and feeling a lot more congenial about my neighbors. She was a quiet woman, although he talked too goddamned much and I thought I'd have to warn Anne, who is a patsy about neighbors not to get too close. He'd be awfully hard to take over a long evening, especially if drinks were served. I didn't really get exactly what his job was—some kind of liaison between training, plans and logistics. I wasn't that much interested. There are all kinds of cutesy-wootsey changes always being made in the permanent base setups. They last until the next colonel comes from Command School.

I opened the door and stopped stock-still.

The FBI guy, Logan, was sitting in the upholstered chair. He was turning the knife over and over in his hands and looking at me with interest.

He spoke first. "Long time, no see, Major."

I put the pie carefully down on the coffee table.

"What the hell are you doing here, Logan?"

"Just checking up on you, Major. Like Colonel Sanders said, you're our pigeon of the week."

I should have been furious; instead I was only utterly tired.

"Okay, you checked. Now blow, I want to get to bed."

He stood up. "Any phone calls, Major?"

"You tell me, Logan. You put a tap on the phone, remember?"

"So I did," he said, "so I did."

He walked past me, stopped and held out the knife.

"Where'd you get this?"

I forced a look of surprise onto my face.

"You mean the knife? I never saw it before in my life. Where did you get it?"

He looked at me deadpan. "You're not going to believe this, Major, but I found it tucked down in the upholstery of that chair over there."

"Really?" I said. "I guess somebody must have given it as a present to one of the kids while I was away."

"Big enough for hunting and fishing, are they?"

"Mad about it."

"It's a good hobby. But you know, Major, I don't think

anybody gave the kids this as a present. Do you happen to know what kind of knife it is?"

"I couldn't care less, frankly, Logan. I've got enough to do learning about weapons like rockets, napalm, etc., that the Air Force dreams up. If they're going to make knives regular issue, I think I'll turn in my papers. People who use knives get too close for comfort, I hear."

"Take a closer look at it," he urged me.

"No, thanks," I said. "I'm off to bed. Just tell me—but the short lecture please. I'm bushed."

"It's a throwing knife," he said. "Russian-made, I think."

"Thanks," I said. "That lets me out of whatever it is you're thinking. I can prove I haven't been anywhere near Russia."

He shook his head dolefully back and forth.

"You know, Major, I can't really make up my mind about you. Just when you get me sold, you start playing cute. Then I start wondering all over again. I hope to God you know what you're doing. You've got an awful lot riding on this deal."

I reached over and ran my thumbnail down the knife blade, then took the weapon out of his hand and stuck it in my back pocket.

I put my index finger right in the middle of his chest. "Just don't you forget what I've got riding on this deal. Don't you forget it for even a minute."

I stared into his eyes for a moment and then turned away.

"Let yourself out, Logan. You know where the door is. And if you don't mind, put the latch on. Some people do really respect locked doors."

I got to my bedroom, before I heard his steps move in the living room. I heard the front door shut and when I looked out the window to see him walking down the flag-stones, I noticed that he had also put the porch light out.

For a moment I wondered if I had done the right thing in not telling him about the attempted knife attack on me. The aggrieved part of me argued: "Why the hell should you? All you represent to him is bait for bigger game." But you don't lead a disciplined life for twelve years without having a healthy respect for constituted authority, and that corner of my mind felt guilty about not reporting the attempted crime.

I guess it was thinking about authority that did it to me. I lay there in the bed for half an hour tossing. I was frantic about Anne and the kids, I was bewildered about the box I had got myself in and I was furious about being a patsy for a pair of cold-blooded government bastards. I was pedaling furiously like a laboratory rat in one of those wire-covered runarounds, looking for a way out, and then I remembered John Hammond. I sat upright in bed, switched on the lamp and reached for the wallet in my trousers pocket. I ran through its slim contents quickly and found the card Hammond had given me. It read like I remembered: "John Wetherill Hammond II, Member of Congress, State of Florida." On the back the vigorous script said: "Thanks, Major, for everything! Give me a ring." I tucked the card carefully back into the wallet, lay back and went to sleep. I had the feeling there was a break in the overcast.

The tailing car picked us up no more than 150 feet from the corner of my house, but I didn't say a word to Mary Ellington. It wasn't necessary. She hadn't stopped talking since she picked me up at the front door, plastic laundry basket and all. I hated to get her involved in the mess, but I couldn't see anything else to do.

She had routed me out of bed at eight thirty in the morning—or rather she had called Anne. I gathered from the tenor of the conversation that the eight-thirty call was a kind of every-other-day ritual between herself and my wife. With her kids and ours safely packed off to school, Mary took the second cup of coffee to the telephone and spent a good half-hour with Anne, putting the finishing touches on a few local reputations.

She hadn't heard from Anne in the forty-eight hours I had been home, but she figured forty-eight hours was enough to take the edge off the reunion and she could resume the beldames' hour, courtesy of Florida Bell.

There had been a pronounced silence when I told her Anne wasn't home. Without actually saying so, I managed to imply that Anne had bundled the kids off to Indian River, where she was sweating out her mother's asthmatic attacks, minor, but annoying.

Mary's got a heart of gold and an open-door policy for the world's afflicted, so it didn't take all that subtlety to get invited to breakfast. Air Force gals run the world's oldest, continuously operating transportation service, covering child emergencies, flight runs, ambulance services, shopping trips, etc. Most of the wives have only one car in the family, so they are accustomed to covering a run for one another. When I told her I hadn't a car, she volunteered that it would only take a few minutes to pick me up.

Her eyes widened a trifle when she saw me on the sidewalk, holding the laundry basket, but she forgot that in a hurry when she screeched to a stop.

I had almost forgotten what a cute trick she was until she burst from the driver's side of the car in scarlet halter, white shorts, lots of golden-tanned skin and no shoes. Mary's the kind of gal they have in mind in the South when they talk about kissing cousins. In about three and a half seconds flat, she had flung herself into my arms, planted a nice soggy kiss roughly near my mouth and hung on like a baby octopus, half-sobbing, half-screaming with joy.

All in all, it was quite a performance and must have given the new neighbors, the Friendlys, an eyeful, if they were looking. I must confess that I was more than a little impressed by the performance myself, until I remembered that Tim Ellington had been away almost as long as I had. I felt a momentary twinge of guilt at my reaction to the warm young body on me, and then I clutched Mary a little harder, fighting back an incipient tear that it wasn't Anne, who is quite a cuddler herself.

Mary talked like a blue jay on a spring morning all the way to her house and I grinned at her without having to say much. When we turned into her driveway, I had no choice. I had to say: "I wonder if you'd mind parking in the garage, Mary? I got a touch of sun in Ubon and the flight surgeon advised me to stay out of the sun as much as possible for a few days."

She looked at me peculiarly. One of her constant quarrels with her husband, Tim, was the fact that she always parked the car outside in the sun and he wanted it in the garage. He's a demon car polisher. She knew I knew all about the quarrels, but she drove the car into the space between the parked toys and the power lawn mower without a word. The excuse was awkward, but it was the only way the rough plan I had in mind would work.

She went through the door connecting the garage to the house and I pretended to fuss with the laundry basket. As I passed round the back of the car toward the connecting door, I snatched down the garage door. I couldn't see where the tailing car was parked, but I was sure it was there.

While I sat at the breakfast table, enjoying the first decent cup of coffee I had since I got back to the States, she fussed over the bacon and eggs. There was a glorious smoky taste to the bacon and the fried eggs were as fresh as the first day of trout-fishing season. I made genuinely appreciative sounds. She poured herself a cup of coffee, lit a cigarette and sat down across the table from me. She tapped a bit of ash into the tray and looked at me with shrewd eyes.

"John Barton McKendrick," she said sharply, "are you and Anne having trouble? Is that what this is all about?"

I was startled for a fraction of a second and a denial rushed to my lips. I realized all of a sudden that this was an easy way out. Mary is an indefatigable do-it-to-her-friends psychiatrist and marriage counselor.

"Well—" I said.

"I knew it, I knew it," she said triumphantly. " I just knew Anne wasn't herself before you came home. She should have been happier than a clam in the mud, I've been saying to myself, and yet she was as jittery as a young girl waiting for the result of the rabbit test. John Barton," she demanded, "what have you been up to?"

I held up my head. "Mary, please don't ask me. I assure

you it's just one of those things. She'll get over it in a few days, I know she will."

"I'm not so sure," she said ominously. "When a nice girl like Anne just walks out on a man without leaving him a note, it's more than just teaching him a lesson; she wants a change in that man, a real change."

An awestruck look came to her eyes as a new thought occurred to her.

"John Barton, you haven't talked divorce, have you?"

I didn't want to overdo it or I'd be there all day.

"Nothing like that, Mary, but it is a little complicated and there are a couple of things I've got to do before Anne and I can get straightened out. Will you help me? No questions asked?"

Her pretty little mouth drew itself into a hard line.

"You're not getting into anything, are you, John Barton? Anything that can hurt Anne any more?"

"No," I said. She was impressed by my sincerity.

"Okay. What do you want me to do?"

"Not much. What's between Anne and me is a service assignment. She doesn't want me to have any part of it. I've got to go through the motions."

There was instant comprehension in Mary's eyes. If the situation were reversed and Tim Ellington were sitting there talking to Anne, there'd be instant understanding in her eyes. All Air force wives suffer from a common disease. They know more about the care and guidance of their husband's career than even the commanding general. It's the one topic of conversation guaranteed to produce a family quarrel.

"I want to make two telephone calls in absolute privacy," I said, "and I want to get out of here without being seen by anyone. You understand, Mary? Anyone!"

"Where do you want to go, John?"

"The Flamingo Shopping Center."

"The Flamingo?" she said in surprise. The Flamingo is a shopping complex, nearly a mile long, maybe the community's busiest.

I held my finger to my lips. "Please, Mary, don't ask me any more. I just can't tell you anything more."

She got a faraway look in her eye and for a moment I wondered if she was turning the whole zany proposition over in her mind. Then she got to her feet briskly.

"The phone's in the living room," she said, "just put your dishes in the sink."

"Where are you going?" I said, puzzled at the sudden switch in mood.

"I can't go to Flamingo Center looking like this, can I?" she asked, pointing to her shorts, and a moment later I heard her clattering up the stairs.

I made the two calls quickly. Hammond's office told me he was definitely expected by ten thirty. I hung up before they could ask my name. I called Mrs. Halloran and she said her husband had told her to expect me, which was a surprise.

I went into the half-bath the Ellington house had, exactly like the one in my own house, and got the uniform out of the laundry basket. I put it on and slipped the tie in place and debated for a moment about wearing the name tag. Then I decided to put it on. If anybody from Logan's office got close to me, he wouldn't need the name tag to identify me.

Mary clacked her way down the stairs in crisp frock and street shoes. I don't know why she worried about the shorts and halter. There wasn't a hell of a lot more cover to the mini skirt she'd changed into and I whistled appreciatively. She was a tasty preview of what I had been missing for the last thirteen months in Uben.

I got into the back of the car and sat on the floor and she looked at me oddly. I was about to give her an explanation when she said with asperity: "I swear to goodness, John Barton, you men are all alike. Let you get away from home for more than a couple of weeks and you lose your manners." I heard the indignant tap of her heels on the concrete floor of the garage and the rattle of the overhead garage door opening.

She backed out of the driveway, turned down a few streets and went sailing down Flamingo Boulevard, chattering away as if the most common thing in her life was carrying on a conversation with a man hiding on the floor in the back of her car. On second thought, I remember that's where my kids were most of the time when Anne was driving, and she had no trouble conversing with them.

I heard the directional signal go on as the car halted.

"Drat that man!" she said angrily.

"What man?" I asked in sudden alarm.

"That fat fool who cut me off," she said. "Men drivers!" She drove for a few seconds, then maneuvered into a parking place.

"You're in front of Herpelsheimer's Department Store," she said. "You'll be safe here. There's a sale on. 'Bye." She hurried off to join the crowd.

I phoned for a cab from the booth near the men's room in Herpelsheimer's and it picked me up as I asked near the rear entrance of the store. I gave the Hallorans' address and the cabdriver gave me a curious look.

"You know that neighborhood, Major?"

I had forgotten what it was still like in the South.

"I know it," I said shortly. "I've got a lot of buddies from Vietnam in the neighborhood."

It was a stupid remark; it obviously called attention to myself, but I had to say it.

The driver averted his eyes from the rearview mirror. "Sorry, sir," he said. "I thought you might be a stranger in town."

We didn't exchange another word till he said "thanks" for the tip in front of the Halloran house. It was like Halloran himself in uniform, everything spruce and squared away.

"Won't you come in, Major?" Mrs. Halloran said. She had a level and direct gaze. I looked at my watch. I had twenty minutes to be at the congressman's office when he got there, which gave me a little time.

She led me into the bright, sunny kitchen and without asking poured me a cup of coffee.

"Have you heard from your wife and children, Major?"

"Nothing," I said.

78

"I'm sorry." She offered me a sweet roll, but I shook my head.

Looking at this grave and courtly lady sitting across the table from me, I decided I had no choice.

"Mrs. Halloran," I said, "you and the sergeant don't have to get involved in this. I can't tell where it will lead—and the government could take a pretty dim view of your helping me. It's not too late. I could leave your car here and pick up a rental."

She smiled at me. "Drink your coffee, Major," she said. "Everybody who's living is involved in other people's problems. At any rate, the decision isn't up to me. Brad already made the decision to help."

"They could bust him," I persisted.

She shrugged. "They could, but sooner or later, life busts everyone, doesn't it, Major?"

She put the car keys in front of me.

"Bring it back whenever you're ready, Major. By the way, Brad phoned. Malone has made the telephone call to Paco."

"How did Brad know I'd be here?" I asked.

"He's a pretty good cop, Major. He told me last night he didn't think you'd just sit around waiting and you'd need transportation."

Even bucking the morning shopping traffic, it took me only a little over six minutes to get to Hammond's office. It was on the second floor of a neighborhood shopping center that included a supermarket, a cleaning store and a liquor store, on a street that I remembered as marking the dividing line between aging middle-class homes and those that were occupied by residents who got increasingly darker the farther they recede from Hammond's office.

It was all very democratic with a small "d." The pretty little black receptionist with Afro-style hair, modified *dashiki* and a black desk sign that identified her as "Thelma Carpenter" was very much on a first name basis with Bobby Joe, the languid blonde secretary who undoubtedly had been told a thousand times she was cute. The walls were a nicely melded melange of previous campaign posters,

79

Small Business Administration announcements offering bright new opportunities, and posters offering more opportunities in the Job Corps, the Peace Corps and the Community Action Corps. There were no recruiting posters for the military, but there was lots of literature on battered and scarred oak tables along the wall.

Thelma was eager to help but doubtful about the chances of seeing the congressman. I gave her Hammond's business card with the invitation to drop in.

She made the three feet to Bobby Joe's desk tentatively. Bobby Joe listened with a frown, nibbling on the end of her ballpoint with tiny baby teeth and staring determinedly at a point four feet above my head. She came to the reception room railing.

"Major," she said, and the frown lines let me know she was personally very distressed, "the congressman is awful busy." I just stared at her in silence. It always works with the lower echelons. In a moment or two, she turned on her heel, walked to a door marked "Robert Kelly" and disappeared.

He came out of his office and he had his hand out even before he had covered the ten feet between us. He pumped my hand, unlatched the little gate on the partition rail and shepherded me into his office before you could say "Office of Economic Opportunity."

"I'm Robert Kelly, the congressman's Number One boy," he said heartily. He tapped a business card with the inscription. "I know he'll want to see you the minute he gets in." He hesitated. "Of course, there are a few urgent things."

"I'll wait, Mr. Kelly." He darted into the outside office. In a minute he was back with a steaming cup of coffee in a paper carton, very much the eager young amateur, serving a distinguished young congressman. He even had the right appearance for it—the beautifully barbered long hair, the mod clothes, the toothy smile. The eyes gave him away, cold, constantly watchful, constantly appraising.

He stood in the doorway of his office, as if a thought had suddenly struck him.

"You know, Major, you could do us a great favor."

I gave him a raised set of eyebrows.

"I just got word the congressman's on his way in. He'll be here in ten minutes and I've got to get my ducks in a row. Would you mind sitting in the next office for a few minutes while I do some busy work? Perhaps you could use these few minutes to get your thoughts in order."

"Thoughts?"

"Sure, what you think of the war, that kind of thing." He looked at me with charming earnestness. "You wouldn't believe the difficulties the Pentagon types make about giving us the real facts about Vietnam. Not," he added hastily, "that you're going to be quoted and nothing that's real security—just a firsthand impression. It will be invaluable to the congressman, invaluable."

I followed his slightly bell-bottomed pants and the cooling coffee into an office next door. I hadn't even sat down before I heard the telephone being dialed behind the door he had carefully closed.

"A very cute one," I murmured to myself.

I met Hammond three years ago on one of those congressional inspection trips that come to foreign bases as regularly as the Fourth of July. They're all alike—inspection trips that manage somehow to require intensive study of the sportier of our allied capitals. The principal inspections consist of studies of the local booze, broads and banquets and they can get pretty hairy. There's something about counterpart funds and foreign accents that bring out the hair on the chest of America's elected representatives.

Pinky Prentice, our base commander in Kyoto, had a knack for these things and he took on most of the congressional packages that the Pentagon sent our way. The reason I got the one that included Hammond was that Pinky had sprained an ankle in a sand trap of a local golf course and fourteen days and nights of flying, dancing and sight-seeing seemed too much even for him.

I turned the junket down flat, until Pinky came up with a public-relations type from a nearby base, who would do the actual bird-dogging, while I confined my skills to flying the plane, laying on the local transportation and doing the morning, noon and evening head count to be certain that we'd gathered up all our sheep from the local whorehouses. It's dirty duty. After the first couple of days on the road, the animals get ugly. There's always a certain amount of ass-kissing required when visiting dignitaries descend on a foreign base, but you can take as gospel Prentice's Law of Visiting Congressmen: "The farther they get from the ballot box, the bigger bastards they become." The average congressman on a foreign base becomes an interesting combination of satyr, boozer and blackmailer, and the really artful ones can upset an entire Air Force base for weeks after an actual visit.

Unlike his midwestern counterpart with a national reputation for treacly oratory and the New England congressman who is noted at home for frugality, Hammond was a gentleman. He took a drink, but he wasn't awash for most of the day and half the nights. He put in a good day's work, mostly listening, which is what he was there for.

He got home reasonably early from most of the state receptions and he and I got in the habit of sharing a mild nightcap. He was an artful questioner and more than once I found myself shocked at how deeply he probed my dissatisfaction and that of most of the airmen in Nam with a war where we are required to keep count of every rocket and bomb we drop, where we must bomb on a flight path 150 yards wide and make most of our bombing passes right into the teeth of massed antiaircraft guns and where a navigational error that takes you a mile into North Vietnam (at 500 mph) can cost you a week's flight pay.

But beneath the congressional suavity, I detected a strange restlessness. I had a date to meet him in a hotel bar in New Delhi and after waiting around a half-hour or so without his showing, I decided to pack it in. As I was putting the key in the door of my hotel room, I heard loud music and high-pitched laughter from Hammond's room next door.

I grinned and thought to myself: "Well, he's finally going to hang one on." Without any thought except ribbing Hammond, I knocked on his door. There was no answer—no diminution in the noise. I tried the door; it was open and I walked in. The sitting room was pretty much of a shambles with much of Hammond's clothing scattered about. I found myself vaguely disappointed and turned back to the door, when, out of the corner of my eye, I noticed his wallet on the floor. I had the feeling he was going to hate himself in the morning if I left it there vulnerable to his visitor's greed and went over, bent down and picked it up.

As I straightened up, I caught a glimpse of his visitor in a mirror behind the partially closed door and stiffened in shock. I walked softly to the door and pushed it open. Hammond was on the bed, clad only in his shorts. Sitting alongside him naked was a beautifully formed young Hindu, gently caressing Hammond's cheek. The dreamy smile on his full red lips did my stomach no good.

My reaction was perhaps gauche, certainly instinctive. I had the young Hindu out of the room in a flash, scrambling into his clothes. I threw him a twenty-dollar bill, a boot in the backside and sent him flying down the hall. I called the security officer of the hotel, warned him that I had found an intruder in my room, described him and made certain that he wouldn't be hanging around for a long time. The New Delhi police take a dim view of natives who roll foreign guests.

Hammond was still snoring away when I picked up his clothing, carefully locked the door and went back to my room. I gave him his wallet in the morning. I told him that it had been turned over to me by the hotel's security officer, who got it from a waiter in the bar.

We never discussed the incident and he made the rest of the trip, sticking pretty close to me. The handwritten message on the business card was the only evidence that we had shared more than fourteen days in a hot, sticky airplane. He had laid the card on top of the souvenir jet helmet with his name printed on it that we give to all the visiting VIPs.

He waved the card in the humid air to let the ink dry and said: "That means what it says, John. Anytime, you need me, for anything."

I had no idea what he could do for me now. Like most Americans, I haven't any idea how much real power a congressman has, but I had some thought that he could take the FBI and Air Force heat off me and possibly, just possibly, he could persuade them that I was innocent till proven guilty and they ought to get cracking and find Anne and the kids.

He came in like an early-season hurricane, slapped me on the back, pumped my hand and grinned like he'd just been told the Rivers and Harbors Committee had awarded a couple of million dollars to his district. Kelly stood in the doorway, approving his performance like a favorite pupil.

"What can I do for you, Major?" Hammond asked eagerly.

I looked at Kelly. "It's private, Mr. Congressman."

Hammond shook his head with a broad smile.

"Nothing doing, Major," he said. "I'm just the front man in this district. Bob's the boy who gets the job done. If you really need something tough, like an invitation to one of the President's prayer breakfasts, Bob's the boy. He knows where the body is buried, where the button is hidden. Believe me, Major, this boy gets it done."

I didn't see that I had any choice, so I laid it out for them, from the time I arrived home till now. I didn't mention Hernandez or Halloran.

As I said before, Hammond was a listener, an artful questioner. He drained the last bit of information out of me, sat back and looked at Kelly. Kelly hadn't said a word through the entire recital.

"What do you think, Bob?"

Kelly didn't mince any words. "It's a real can of worms. How far do you trust McKendrick?" He asked the question as if I weren't there.

"As far as I trust you," Hammond said quietly.

Kelly nodded. "Okay." He turned to me. "What do you want from us, Major?"

"Find my wife and kids—or get somebody to find them. I'll sweat out the business of the ring. I just want them safe."

"Can we put any heat on the FBI, Bob?" asked Hammond. "I find it totally incredible that they're just sitting back, waiting for party or parties unknown to move."

"Christ, John," Kelly said dubiously, "I don't know. The FBI has got this raw evidence thing and they use it like it's real."

Hammond explained: "The Bureau has managed to remain virtually untouched, even by congressional investigations. Their constant reply to questions is that they merely collect evidence about people, they don't evaluate it. People who get accused of being Communists, for example, are never accused by the FBI; the Bureau merely says that in questioning people, the allegation is made."

"Can you get to Hoover? Directly?" I asked. "I mean, a congressman has a lot of influence."

Kelly shook his head at me. "No, such a question is always sent back through channels. You'd wind up talking to Logan. Frankly, Major, even if we could go to Hoover, I'd think a half-dozen times before we did it. I don't want the congressman eyeball to eyeball with the head of the FBI. It wouldn't do his image with the voters any good. Most Americans think of Hoover as untouchable."

I looked at him with disgust. "Then you can't do anything?"

Kelly shrugged. Hammond got to his feet, paced the office. He was obviously thinking hard. He snapped at Kelly: "Get Arnie Johnson of Haverford's on the phone. Ask him if the appraisal of the jewel will stand up. Don't let him give you that security crap. I want to know if the whole story is a phony."

It didn't take Kelly long; he got the jewelry store on the phone, got connected to Johnson, asked his question. I could see from his lengthening face that we weren't going to get any help from that quarter. He hung up.

"Arnie says the appraisal is sound. If anything, he was a bit low on his guess about the value."

Hammond nodded, as if he knew it all the time. He looked at me keenly. "I must ask one question, Major. Are you clean on this thing?"

"As God is my judge," I said.

"Good," he said. "Get me Effie Graham," he ordered Kelly.

"Hold it a minute, boss," said Kelly. "What are you planning?"

Hammond grinned broadly. "There just may be another way of putting a torch to the FBI's backside." He turned to me: "I've got a speech today before the FDR, the Florida Daughters of the Republic; they're a kind of combination minor league Daughters of the American Revolution and garden club. They're very big for patriotism—and azaleas. You come along with me to the luncheon. Bob will alert the newspapers and we'll have you photographed with Effie and me. The evening papers will carry the photograph—you can fix that, can't you, Bob?—and unless I miss my guess, Mr. Logan will be on the horn to Washington minutes later pointing out that I'm now aware of what's going on. It just may move them to action; at any rate, it's going to give them some pause before they push you around again."

"I don't like it," Kelly said quickly. "Suppose it turns out they've got something on McKendrick"—he looked at me quickly—"I don't mean you're guilty, McKendrick, but suppose they make it look like that, then the congressman's going to be in a hell of a spot."

"Stop looking under the bed," said Hammond. "I told you I trust this man as much as I trust you. I also owe him. I've taken a lot of chances with you on a hell of a lot less evidence. Get Effie on the phone."

I was bitterly disappointed. I wanted a wife and kids back. They were playing public-relations games. It seemed to me that Hammond had rather neatly euchred me and got himself some votes in the process. I could see the caption on the photo that would appear as promised in the evening papers: "Returned Vietnam pilot guest of FDR and Congressman Hammond." In Kelly's words, the picture wouldn't do the congressman's image any harm. If at a later date something went wrong, the congressman could throw me to the wolves, piously proclaiming that he was shocked by the sudden turn of events.

It was a slender straw he was offering me, but it was the only straw in town. So I grimaced my way through the photo session with Mrs. Graham and excused myself shortly, mumbling something about security. She was a nice middle-aged lady with startling blue hair who was very understanding that I was a bombful of military secrets that might be spilled inadvertently at the lunch. She gave me a bunch of flowers to take home to Anne and increased the already overwhelming level of decibels among her fellow members by leading the applause as I left. How they managed it with such a firm grip on their second Manhattans I never will figure out.

I let myself into the gravelike quiet of the house. The telephone remained stubbornly silent while I fixed myself a fried egg sandwich with a glass of milk. I lifted the receiver once or twice to see if I could detect the wiretap. Mickey Spillane is dead wrong. I couldn't detect the telltale buzzing he says is there. Either that or Florida telephone service is just as bad as people say it is.

When you've sweated out as many flight lines as I have, the reflex becomes automatic. When you wait, you lie down on the floor and go to sleep. I did. I don't have any idea how long I'd been there on the floor alongside the phone when its harsh jangle woke me out of the nap.

My response was sleepy but prompt. "Major McKendrick's residence."

"Paco Hernandez here." The voice was that of a high-pitched high school dropout with a Latin flavor. "Your friend called me. Said I could help."

"You can, Mr. Hernandez. I'm planning a party—with lots of native food. He thought you could help get me some *Café Beneficia*. I'll need eight pounds of green beans."

The contempt came through the telephone line with total clarity.

"Ain't nobody in Spickville going to give you eight

pounds," he said. "Five's about the most you can get this time of the year, particularly when you need it in a hurry."

"I'm sorry, Mr. Hernandez," I said firmly. "If I can't get eight, then I guess I'll have to look elsewhere. I'd hate to see you lose out on the commission."

"You're paying commission?" he asked. He sounded a little tense.

"Of course. I know you'll have a lot of trouble rounding up eight pounds. I'll pay twelve per cent."

He may have been a high school dropout, but he knew his fractions.

"Fifteen," he said.

"Twelve," I said, "the absolute top."

"I ought to get something extra for picking up the merchandise," he said plaintively.

"No need," I said. "I'll pick it up myself." I wondered did this little thief think I was really going to turn a $33,000 emerald over to him?

He didn't. He was just operating on the old principle, never give a sucker an even break. Now that he understood the facts, his voice shrank to its basic small-time whine.

"I'll call you back."

"In an hour, Mr. Hernandez," I said.

I figured I'd have to give Logan's people something more to chew on, so I went out to the garage and got out the fancy barbecue unit that Anne had bought before I went away. As I expected, it was covered with grease and still had the ashes of the last fire in it.

I took it out to the front of the house, turned on the hose, make a bucket of suds and started grinding away with a steel-wire brush and some soap pads. It took Hernandez almost the full hour before he called back.

"I can get you eight pounds of the green beans," he said.

"Fine," I said. "I've got a hankering for Spanish food. I'll be at Timeo's at Eighth and Figueroa at eight o'clock. I ought to be finished about eight thirty. Why not join me then and we can have a cup of coffee together?"

I hung up quickly. I didn't want him to argue. I had no

stomach for an assignation in some dark alley. At Timeo's there's a door from the kitchen to a tiny parking lot that handles the overflow from the main parking lot on busy Saturday nights. I planned to leave Halloran's car conspicuously in the front parking lot to occupy Logan's boys.

I debated whether I'd call Halloran, then turned the idea down. I assumed that Hernandez was keeping an eye on Paco and that he and Halloran were touching base. I had a couple of hours to fill. I used them to mow and trim the lawn, to try to get some order out of the chaos that two boys and a healthy young girl can make of a combination garage and storage room. After all my worry about Anne and the kids, it sounds ridiculous that I blew my top when I saw the way the kids had left my tool chest. It was a lovely mess of gouged chisels, rusty wrenches, fouled fishing line and tackle. In the middle of my first burst of profanity, I remembered and cooled down.

I felt the sweat running down my brow and my chest and for a while as I hacked and clipped and pruned, I was able to pretend that I was an ordinary father with a busy day off.

I scrubbed myself over and over again in the shower, then slipped into a pair of slacks and a sports shirt. I rummaged through the storage bags and found the seersucker jacket I was looking for and tried it on. I had lost about twelve pounds in Ubon and the coat hung as loosely as I hoped. But there was still no place to conceal the knife, where it wouldn't cut the worn material or drag the jacket down. I stripped off the coat and bound the knife with adhesive tape to the inside of my left arm, between wrist and elbow. It was awkward, I knew, but I thought I could get at it in a hurry by sliding my right hand down the inside of the left sleeve and yanking it. The only trouble was that when I tried it, it didn't work. It tore the bejesus out of the hair on my left arm, and the adhesive remained remarkably adhesive and tough. I tried it a couple of times and unless El Rojo and his boys had been on Medicare for the last ten years, I wouldn't have had time to get at the knife. Feeling silly as hell, I rummaged through the drawers of our bedroom chest and found a pair of winter stretch socks, put them on and slipped the knife into the top of the right sock. Like every other form of advertised American progress, the stretch socks did indeed stretch, but they didn't hold the knife very securely. I had to settle for a rubber band around the top of the sock and hope I'd have plenty of time if there came any occasion to use the knife. "Come to think of it," I told myself, "if I've got all that time, why don't I call a cop?"

With that very sensible thought, I went out to dinner.

# 8

Timeo's isn't much on decor and to tell the truth, the food isn't much either—lots of black bean soup, a couple of varieties of chicken and an occasional bit of fish. But they are long on two things, extraordinary courtesy and perhaps the finest Mexican beer in the world. The combination of warmth and icy cold are like the sweet and sour in Pennsylvania Dutch cooking and they add up to a pleasant meal.

Timeo is too fat, but his five feet eight and 220 pounds are carried with dignity and grace. He asked for the children and Anne, regretted they weren't with me, recommended the arroz con pollo and brought me a marvelously chilled beer and a frosted glass.

I ate hungrily and the second beer appeared precisely as I was draining the last of the first. Timeo returned in a moment with a frown on his face.

"A gentleman is asking for you, Major," he said in a tone that left no doubt that he didn't think the visitor was a gentleman, nor that a customer who had enjoyed his hospitality ought to be meeting this character here.

"Thank you, Timeo," I said. "I've been expecting him. A matter of business. Coffee for two, please."

He frowned at me for a moment, then the unemotional cast returned to his face and he turned and snapped his fingers at a figure in the arched stucco doorway.

Paco Hernandez looked like one of the chorus boys in a third-rate version of *West Side Story*, slim and slightly reptilian. The glossy black hair touched the collar of his orange sports jacket, and his eyes slid malevolently over his shoulder and he said, "Spick bastard" to Timeo's retreating back.

"Got the merchandise?" he asked. His eyes kept sliding round the tables nearest us. It wasn't curiosity, I suddenly realized. It was fear.

"It's here, if you can get me the eight pounds," I said.

I saw the greedy battle in his eyes as he tried to decide if he could screw me out of a few more bucks. Fear won out.

"Yeah, you get the eight. I get a flat thousand or no deal." It was forty bucks more than the 12 per cent I promised him, but it didn't seem important.

"Where do I meet your man and when?"

He looked at his watch. "In ten minutes," he said. "You go through the back parking lot, down the alley to Figueroa. It's the second house on the left, Number 84. Papa's office is on the first floor."

"Office?" I asked in surprise.

"Sure," he said loftily. "Papa's a businessman. You think he works out of a loft or something, like a goddamned junkman?"

"And I get the eight right away?"

He looked at me in disgust.

"Of course not," he said. "You think Papa's some frigging bank or loan company? You show him the merchandise, he makes a phone call, a messenger brings the dough to his office. You leave there, come to the back parking lot, give me my cut and that's all there is to it. I'll be here waiting for you at ten o'clock."

He shoved his chair away from the table abruptly and left. Timeo watched him thread his way through the diners, followed him through the archway to the door as if to make certain he was really gone, went to the cashier and frostily brought me my check.

I invited him to join me in a brandy and after the barest possible hesitation, he sat down.

"To your safe return," he toasted me. I was pleased. I hadn't been sure he'd known I was away or even interested.

"To old friends," I said in return. I drank my brandy at a gulp, saw Timeo's eyes widen slightly and then he rose to his feet. I turned to see what had attracted his attention.

Robert Kelly, Congressman Hammond's Number One boy, was coming to the table. He had a newspaper under his arm.

"Major McKendrick," he said, shaking hands. "Timeo." Timeo was smiling at him indulgently, the smile of the patron for an old and valued guest.

Kelly handed me the paper. "As promised," he said. The picture of the congressman, Effie and myself stared back at me. The caption was just what I thought it was going to be. Kelly crossed his fingers and nodded at me: "Here's hoping."

Timeo craned over my shoulder.

"How nice," he said. "I admire the congressman; I am glad that you and he know each other." He turned to Kelly. "This picture is significant?"

"Who knows?" he said. "Major McKendrick is a distinguished military officer and the friend of important people like the congressman. He has been a base commander, served also with the Marines and has been more than a little bit of a hero in Vietnam."

Timeo snapped his fingers, a bottle of brandy appeared on the table and three glasses swiftly filled.

"To courage," he said simply, and I found myself blushing with pleasure. I couldn't find anything to say, so I just finished my drink. Kelly took only a sip from his.

"Excuse me, won't you?" he said, smiling. "But a politician's work is never done. Your people have many needs," he said to Timeo.

"The congressman has already done many things for our people," Timeo said gravely. "We are grateful."

I was afraid Timeo might want to chat after Kelly disappeared, but a somewhat tipsy party commanded his attention. After the initial frown at the sudden noisy babble, he put the proprietary smile on his face, murmured "*Vaya con Dios,* Major," and hurried to his guests.

I stepped into the men's room for a minute. I told myself I wanted to check on the knife in my sock. The fact is I wasn't at all that eager to venture into the dark night beyond the parking lot. I told myself on the plus side that everything was going approximately according to Captain Hernandez' plan. The louder argument came back from the minus side of my mind and it said: "It sure is. He's setting you up like a sitting duck and here you are going up against kidnapers and murderers and all you have is a knife." The argument was so out of accord with common sense that I scurried, rather than walked through the back door, into the parking lot before my nerve ran out altogether.

I paused in the shadow of a car and peered into the intense darkness of the parking lot to adjust my night vision. I wondered about Kelly. What the hell was all that stuff about war hero, etc., he was giving Timeo. I knew Kelly didn't like me any better than I liked Captain Hernandez. Maybe Kelly felt I was setting Hammond up for another fall guy like myself.

I looked as deeply into the alley as possible. I saw nothing, heard nothing except the tiny scuffle of a possible rat near a garbage can. I walked while the sweat under my arms ran like ice water down my sides. I put my back against the wall and scuttled along to Figueroa Street.

There were six stone steps up to the front door of the second house from the corner and I sprinted up them and through the glass door at the head of the stairs. I was breathing a lot more heavily than the exertions required. The front door led into a small vestibule and a locked door beyond. I looked around for a buzzer and saw the names on the mailboxes. Mendoza was the name of the one in the middle and I pushed the little red button under the nameplate. The buzz came instantaneously and I entered, heard the door lock behind me. It was a long steep flight of carpeted stairs. I was glad it was well lit. The door facing the landing was steel, painted to resemble a grained wood. I knocked, heard a chain unbolted and the door swung open.

"Major McKendrick," said a voice, "do come in." I stepped forward. The door closed noiselessly behind me and I turned. The man at the door was a huge Negro; he had an ugly scar from the edge of his hair right down to his chin line. He was bare-chested, barefooted and unarmed if you didn't count a gleaming machete that in the soft light of the room looked honed to razor sharpness. He didn't look at me but over my shoulder. I turned: "Mr. Mendoza?"

The little man behind the desk rose and smiled. It was a smile of honeyed sweetness. He was puzzlingly familiar and I ran through the memory cards in my mind for some identification. Then it struck me. There is a statue in one of the ancient Franciscan missions in San Antonio of Junipero Serra, the famed missionary. Mendoza had the same gentle face, just barely lined with age, the same liquid eyes, the tiny fringes of gray hair on the sides and back of the head, like a tonsure. I remembered also that Fra Serra had been tough enough to climb mountains, traverse thousands of miles alone and to defy almost all forms of authority.

"Come sit with me, my son," he said. The voice has a soft resonance. I could almost imagine it comforting me from behind the screen in a confessional. Reluctantly I moved to the chair he indicated.

He had a quizzical smile on his face.

"Did you expect a Latin version of Shylock?" he asked. I had been thinking exactly that.

"I fear Captain Hernandez has been telling romantic stories about me again," he said ruefully. At the mention of the police captain's name, I came erect with alarm.

Mendoza shook his head dolefully.

"Did you imagine, Major, that I could survive in this city, all these years, without being able to see through so transparent a plot? But I must confess it was done artfully with Paco Hernandez and the good Sergeant Halloran."

He reached into a side drawer of his desk. The large box he lifted onto the desk was exquisitely made of old Spanish oak cunningly inlaid with silver.

"Lovely, isn't it, Major?" he said, pointing to the box. "It is fourteenth-century Spanish. Tradition has it that it once belonged to Ponce de León. The silver tracery is a representation of *arbor vitae,* 'the tree of life.' The connection with de León's 'fountain of youth' is of course obvious. I have no reason to know if the story is authentic. You would not believe, Major, the incredible stories people tell me when they seek to dispose of something valuable."

He took an intricately wrought silver key from a ring on his watch chain, opened the case and took out one of the loveliest decanters I've ever seen—a kind of luminous cloud-blue.

"The decanter," he said gently, "is sixteenth-century Venetian. Authentic. So, thank God, is the brandy."

He raised his eyebrows, and the huge Negro brought a tray with three glasses on it. Mendoza filled them carefully, handed me one, another to the Negro and took the third. He raised his glass, inclined his head gravely and said: "Welcome back to America, Major. I am sorry you could not have returned under better circumstances."

I drank.

"Then you don't want the ring?" It was all I could think to say.

His eyes opened wider. "On the contrary, I want it very much, Major. I hope nothing I have said has persuaded you to the contrary."

I must have looked my bewilderment.

He held his hand out and I placed the ring in his palm. It was woman soft and the fingernails were beautifully manicured. He placed the ring on the desk without examining it.

"I think you had better understand me, Major. Perhaps it will help if you disabuse yourself of the notions you received from Captain Hernandez. He called me, I am sure, a fence, or perhaps even other names more disagreeable. In

95

a way, I suppose it is true, but I prefer to think of my role in the community as being somewhat more significant."

He made a signal and the Negro refilled the glasses.

"It is interesting, Major," he said musingly, "to think that this area, St. Petersburg and its environs, has been settled for more than three hundred years. In all that time, the Latins—it makes no difference if they're Spanish, Mexican, Cuban or Negro in origin—have been poor, desolately poor.

"The poor, the good Lord says, are always with us. Where there is the poor, there is stealing. And this is as it should be. If a man has no hope of anything for himself and his family, how can he respect the property rights of others? He does not know such a thing. It is incomprehensible. So, if the poor steal from the rich, who can blame them, Major? But if the poor steal from the poor, then dreadful things—crimes of violence can result. It is here where I am valuable to the community. I maintain a marketplace, day and night, year in and year out, depression or prosperity, for the poor, so that violence shall be contained. I have explained this often to Captain Hernandez, but that poor harried man does not see the concept clearly. I think, though, Sergeant Halloran does."

"My ring, Mr. Mendoza?" I said politely.

"Oh yes," he said. He took a jeweler's loupe from the desk and scrutinized the ring.

"Superb," he said. "Of course, the setting is nothing, but the stone, it is of the highest quality."

"You'll let me have the eight thousand dollars?"

A look of pain crossed his face. "You Americans take much of the pleasure out of business. You have no talent for bargaining. We will reach an agreement shortly, Major. Do not fear. First I must tell you why I want the ring."

I lit a cigarette and a pained look returned to his face. "Isn't life hazardous enough, Major, without inflicting needless risk on yourself?" He shook his head. "Forgive me, sir. I grow crotchety about things like cigarettes as I grow older." He glanced down at the ring.

"Major," he said, and I sat up straighter at the sharp

intensity of tone, "Major, someone killed one of my people, Frank Martinez, and I want to know why."

"You mean," I said in surprise, "Frank Martinez, the policeman, worked for you?"

"You miss my point. Martinez, all policemen, and I are in the same business maintaining a delicate balance between law and order. Martinez was killed brutally by some stranger to the community."

"The crushed hands?"

He nodded in agreement. "Yes, there are rumors that a person called El Rojo, who directs these things, may have committed the crime himself. The point is, Major, I cannot permit outside violence to happen without some action. I have a business that is vulnerable to such intrusions. In addition, I had a feeling for Martinez. He was a good man at his job, and the community needs such people."

The philosophy might be interesting, but it was his problem. I asked my question directly: "Can you tell me anything about my wife and children?"

"No, Major, I cannot." He sounded regretful. "That bothers me too. It seems that a crime against a defenseless woman and her children is among the ugliest crimes of civilization. But it concerns me more, Major, because I have no information of your wife and children. As an experienced soldier, you know that information is the lifeblood of a fighting force."

He pointed to the emerald glittering on the table.

"Captain Hernandez is right. It is clear that the ring is a vital factor in the violence and the possible crimes. I agree with him that moving it out of its predestined channels may bring my enemies, yours, to the surface. Yes, I will buy your ring."

"How much?"

"Please," he said, "the bargaining is a vital part of the business. Let me make a phone call, secure a sufficient quantity of cash to suit both our needs. Would you mind waiting in the other room, Major?"

He nodded to the Negro, and I left the room. The Negro

led me to a small book-lined room, with a desk and contour chair. The books were leather-bound classics, and a whole shelfful of books on criminology. I paced the floor restlessly. The window was iron-shuttered, securely braced, with an opening of only two inches. By pressing my face against the edge of either shutter, I could see half the length of Figueroa Street. I was about to turn away from the window, when I saw a figure move stealthily out from the house directly opposite Papa Mendoza's. I snapped out the lights, stared into a dark corner of the library to readjust my night vision and went back to the window. The orange coat glowed softly; it was Paco Hernandez.

I had expected something like this; he was too much the petty thief not to attempt a simple holdup, probably with a couple of street-gang members at ready call.

I knocked at the door of Papa Mendoza's room.

"Come in, Major," said the soft voice.

"I was looking out the window—" I began.

"You saw Paco Hernandez?" He smiled. "I have sent Philippe, my Negro friend, to send him away. He will go —of that you may be sure. Paco is a greedy one—and you might have made a nice handy pigeon. Sit down, Major, let us haggle. Such a lovely word."

For all Papa's talk, there wasn't much haggling. He had spent too many years with clients over a barrel to have any ideas about generosity. The offer came down, as Captain Hernandez had predicted, to $5,000. When I protested that I had to pay Paco $1,000 in commission, leaving me with a net of only $4,000, he responded predictably too.

"I will be fair to you, Major. I am sure that after his encounter with Philippe, Paco will agree that he has not acted suitably in this matter. We will therefore cut his commission to $500. I will pay you $5,500. Thus you will net $5,000—or a clear gain of $1,000 over my previous offer." He was smugly confident he had a patsy. "Take a few minutes to think it over, Major."

I got up from the table, walked into the other room. I didn't bother to put on the lights. I was merely going through the motions and Papa knew it. I glanced through the slit in the iron shutters. Paco was gone—but there was suddenly something new in the picture. Two cars glided around the corner, with only their parking lights on. They stopped a respectable distance from Mendoza's house, and the parking lights suddenly snapped off.

I watched them curiously. I had the idea that they were Papa Mendoza's people, with the second car riding shotgun on the messenger with the money. Two men got out of the first car and walked to the second. At that distance and in the uncertain light, I could be wrong, I knew. But I saw the long hair, the confident swagger, and I was certain that one of the men was Bob Kelly, Congressman Hammond's assistant. For a moment, I thought I recognized the second man, something about the walk, the set of the shoulders, but he quickly disappeared in the shadows of the second car. I pulled back from the window. Even the dim light from the street lamppost was destroying my visual concentration. I stared into a dark corner of the little room, for the fifteen seconds the night fighter's manual recommended, and turned back to the window. The first car was gone; there was no movement in the second car. I puzzled Kelly's presence in the neighborhood, but the insistent hall buzzer sounding in Papa's office drove the thought from my mind.

Papa's haggling had made him smugly confident, too confident.

"Will you come in, Major," he called. "The money has arrived."

I walked into his office, blinding in the light. Papa was lucky. The man who burst through the door with the gun in his hand plunged head on into me and we both went down in a tangle of legs and arms. The force of his lunge drove me into Papa's desk. I had a glimpse of the man rolling onto his stomach and bracing his gun with his left arm. It looked as big as a .75-millimeter cannon. I lashed out with a leg and jarred his arm. I had a momentary regret that I had forgotten the knife tucked into the sock on that same leg. The man scrambled after the gun on the floor. He didn't reach it. Philippe, the huge Negro, scuttled through the door, hit him smartly with a leather-covered blackjack. The man gave a convulsive kick and sprawled facedown on the floor. The Negro didn't give him a second look but turned to the door and carefully locked it.

"That was very careless, Papa," he said disapprovingly.

"It was indeed, Philippe," Mendoza said. He came around the desk. "Are you all right, Major?"

"A little confused," I said, climbing to my feet. "What's it all about?"

Without answer, he moved over to the man on the floor, made a small gesture, and the huge Negro turned the man over and went through his pockets. He had nothing on him but a few dollars and a pack of cigarettes. Papa Mendoza ripped open the pack of cigarettes, sniffed deeply and handed them to Philippe.

The huge Negro inhaled, nodded and bent over the man again. He turned him over on his face, ran his fingers round the belt line. He came up with a wickedly gleaming knife, remarkably like the one I myself had forgotten in my sock.

"Cuban," said Papa after a quick examination of the blade. He walked over and sat down heavily behind his desk. Mechanically he filled the brandy glasses again and handed them round. Almost as an afterthought, he took a pair of handcuffs from a side drawer, gave them to Philippe, who snapped them round the wrists of the man on the floor. The man moaned slightly.

"I have been careless in more than the door," Papa said thoughtfully. "I underrated Paco completely; he was more greedy than I thought. Undoubtedly he was seeking three commissions—from you, from me and from the people who sent this man."

"Fidelistas?" asked Philippe.

"I should think so—the knife, the marijuana," said Mendoza. He looked at the man on the floor like he was an interesting bag of merchandise to be opened at leisure.

"We shall find out soon enough."

"Do you think he will talk?" I asked. "My wife and children—"

"He will talk," Mendoza said coldly. "About your wife and children—if he knows, he will tell us. Philippe will guarantee that. But I am not remembering my manners, Major, I have not thanked you for saving my life."

He raised his glass in salute. "I am in your debt, Major."

"All I did was get in the way," I said.

"The face of Providence has many aspects," he said softly. "Now, Major, if you'll just take your money and go. Philippe and I have much to do."

The man on the floor groaned. Mendoza didn't even pause in counting the money into a pile on the desk. Philippe idly kicked the Cuban in the kidney. After the quick gasp of pain, the man subsided.

"Count it if you will, Major," Mendoza said. "Philippe, would you go downstairs and see that the street is clear?"

Philippe handed him the gun and slipped through the door. I counted out the pile—it came to $5,500 in fifty- and twenty-dollar bills.

"I should not give Paco a commission if I were you, Major," Mendoza said. "You may tell him that I do not wish him to have it. I will settle with him later."

The restless move of the slim finger down the edge of the blade made me feel a moment's sympathy for poor greedy Paco.

"You'll let me know what you find out about my wife and children?" I asked.

He looked at me with mounting impatience. "Please, Major, do not waste time. Philippe and I have much to do."

The Negro stood in the doorway. I followed him down the stairs, waited in the hallway as he requested, until he came back from the street.

"There is no one in sight," he said. "I should go quickly if I were you." But he put a restraining hand on my chest. "A moment, Major. I too must express my thanks for saving the life of Papa Mendoza. The debt will be repaid." He ran lightly up the stairs and I grasped the front door.

I couldn't help it. I suppose I would have been safer in the shadows of Figueroa Street, but I walked precisely on the curbing, one hand on my money, one hand filled with the knife. Strangely enough, I felt safer in the darkness of the alley leading to Timeo's back parking lot. Once again I slid along the wall, waited for a moment at the mouth of the alley, then raced on tiptoe to the nearest car, slouched down behind it and held my breath, listening for the sound of possible pursuers. I counted to twenty, then forced myself to count to twenty again, before I started to slide round the car.

"Hold it!" a voice rasped, and something hard was shoved into my back and the beam of a flashlight hit me in the face. I froze.

"Hands on the top of the car," the voice behind me commanded. I put my hands on the car and the knife tumbled to the ground with a tinny clink on the macadam. Big rough hands ran up and down my body.

"He's clean, Captain." Relief surged through me as I recognized the heavy timber of Halloran's voice.

"Turn round, McKendrick," ordered the other voice.

I turned as slowly as I could. Hernandez didn't relax the aim of the gun for a moment. It was square in the middle of my belly.

"Move out, McKendrick," said Hernandez. "Right around the car and into Timeo's." Halloran stepped aside and fell into step with Hernandez, behind me. I couldn't understand what the hell it was all about.

They herded me past the back door, pushed me into the men's room and bolted the door. It would make a pretty problem for Timeo's customers.

"What the hell are you doing here, McKendrick?" snapped Hernandez. He had holstered the gun, but the anger was showing in his face.

"Just what you expected, Captain," I said. "I turned the ring over to Papa Mendoza, took my dough and came back to pick up Halloran's car. Hell, you know that! At least you ought to know it, if you'd been watching like I thought you were."

They exchanged glances. I couldn't make out any meaning in them.

"You mean you didn't notice anything unusual in the parking lot?" Hernandez' disbelief was so evident it didn't matter what I answered.

"No. Should I have seen something?"

"Empty your pockets."

I handed everything over to Halloran. He skipped the odd change, the cigarettes and the lighter, riffled through the roll of bills.

"Fifty-five hundred bucks," he told Hernandez. "He did tell the truth about that. He did sell the ring."

"Put it back in his pockets," said Hernandez. "Bring him along outside." He led the way through the back door to the parking lot. We came to the car where they had picked me up and he shoved the flashlight into my hand.

"Take a look for yourself." He gave me a few feet of room but not enough so that I could make a break for it, even if his set face hadn't persuaded me that was a bad idea. I played the flashlight on the car and caught my breath. It was a blue Ford station wagon, with the familiar beat-up 1964 look. I started to slide round the car to get into the driver's seat. Halloran blocked my way.

"Try the other side, Major," he said softly.

So I got in on the other side and switched on the dome light. I needn't have. Even in the dark, I could have found the familiar dents and scratches. It was my car—Anne's car —the one that had been missing from the garage—the one that Sam, the short-order cook out on the bay, had said he'd seen hightailing out of Tampa.

"How'd it get here?" The question came hoarsely out of a suddenly dry throat.

"You tell us, Major," said Hernandez. His tone was every bit as belligerent as that of Colonel Sanders when he said the identical words to me in the Officers' Club.

"Anne—the kids, what about them?"

103

Hernandez glared at me; Halloran merely shrugged.

"No sign, Major," said the sergeant.

I screwed my way around in the seat. There was the usual mess—half-broken toys, a few comic books, the nearly empty Kleenex box. I looked at the debris and an overwhelming feeling of disaster came over me. I gripped the steering wheel until my knuckles whitened to keep the emotion back.

"What does it mean—the car here?"

They watched me silently and I beat the seat with my fist in frustration. Then I noticed the crumpled bag under the driver's seat. I reached down. The bag was warm. I started to open it, when Hernandez' hard hand fell on my wrist.

"Hold it, right there, Major," and he reached inside the bag and brought out a few half-eaten pieces of pizza.

He held them out to Halloran. "Still warm, Sergeant." I took a closer look at the messy bits of food.

"May I?" I asked, and reached for one of the pieces. I stuck it under Hernandez' nose. "I'm right," I said excitedly. "Shane's been in the car and not more than two hours ago."

"You can tell your son has been in the car just from looking at a piece of pizza?" he asked sceptically.

"Sure. Anne told me he's missing two front teeth. He would leave that kind of pattern on toast. Right, Sergeant?"

Halloran screwed his eyes up thoughtfully.

"Could be, Captain," he said. "That boy's got a hole in his front teeth big enough to drive a jeep through. Could be he'd eat like that."

A look of doubt again appeared on Hernandez' face. "Out this way, McKendrick," he ordered me. I slid off the seat and he moved round the car ahead of me. He stopped me at the bumper on the driver's side.

He shone the flashlight down the driver's side of the car. I took a look and pushed away from him and got sick. The flashlight beam hadn't been all that strong—it didn't have to be. It was strong enough to show me a picture that would take me a week of Sundays to forget. The body beside the car was Paco's. There wasn't much blood; most of it had been absorbed by the orange sports jacket, in an obscene dark stain that welled from the knife, deeply imbedded in the lower left-hand side of the slim body. The left hand, the only one I saw in the beam of the flashlight, looked like it was encased in an oversized mitten. I knew it wasn't a mitten, even in the flickering light. The hand had been stamped into the pavement. I didn't want to see the other one under the body of the car. I took a deep breath and put my hand out for support on the bumper.

"Take the goddamned light out of my face, Hernandez," I said harshly, and turned on my heel.

"Where are you going?" he asked.

"Home," I said shortly. "Even you're not stupid enough to think I killed Paco. First of all, I wasn't here. You can check with Papa Mendoza; secondly, I couldn't have known my car was here, and third, what the Christ are you standing around here for? Now we know my wife and kids are back in town. Get off your ass and find them!"

I strode angrily back to Timeo's. I was furious and excited. There was a moment's hesitation and then I heard the footsteps behind me. "Hold up a minute, Major," said Halloran soothingly, grabbing my arm as I reached the door. I shook him off and walked to the bar. The restaurant was empty except for an aging waiter dozing at a table near the front door.

The bartender looked up warily as I approached the bar.

"Double Scotch," I snapped. He hesitated and then started to make the drink. I looked behind me. Timeo was standing in the middle of the room, a look of concern on his face. He was looking at Hernandez and Halloran. Finally he made up his mind, moved behind the bar and said something in a low voice to the bartender.

The bartender walked over to the waiter by the front door, whispered to him, locked the door, snapped a switch, and the entrance lights went off. Both of them disappeared into the kitchen without a glance at any of us.

Timeo waited till the sound of their footsteps died down.

"There is trouble, Captain Hernandez?" he asked.

"Sí."

"For my friend Major McKendrick or for me?"

Hernandez shrugged. "Who knows? Paco Hernandez lies dead in the back parking lot with a throwing knife in his back."

"The Lord have mercy on his soul," said Timeo, crossing himself rapidly. "I did not like him," he said seriously. "He was a bad one. But I know nothing of it."

"Did you see anyone, a stranger perhaps, come into the restaurant from the back entrance?" asked Hernandez.

"From the back entrance? None that I noticed. From the front entrance, many. They were I would say tourists. Timeo's is not unknown."

"Fidelistas?"

Timeo's hands were thrown out. "Again, Captain, who knows? There are rumors—" He let the sentence trail off.

"But none such familiar to you?"

Timeo drew himself up, stiff with dignity.

"It is well known that my sympathies do not include Fidelistas, Captain, but I serve such guests as come into my restaurant."

Hernandez nodded in understanding.

"It is a troubled world, Timeo," he said absently but sympathetically.

I wondered how I could ask my own question without tipping my hand. There seemed nothing but the direct approach.

"By the way, Timeo," I said, "did Bob Kelly, the congressman's assistant, come back into the restaurant after I left?"

Hernandez' head turned alertly.

"Kelly? What's he got to do with you?"

I saw a copy of the evening newspaper open on the end of the bar. I got up, turned to the photo of Hammond and me and laid it in front of Hernandez. He read the caption and looked at me with raised eyebrows.

"I met Hammond in the East," I said. "We got to be friends. I thought he could keep the FBI off my back. He didn't seem anxious to get into my hassle—but he did arrange for this publicity picture. He thought the FBI would get the word I had an in with him and they'd go easier. I had an idea Kelly might have some word on the Bureau's reaction."

"Politicians!" muttered Hernandez.

"Kelly did come in about nine thirty," said Timeo. "He did not mention you; merely had a brandy and left." He hesitated. "Captain? There will not be any unfavorable publicity?"

"There will not," Hernandez said emphatically. "There is no reason one so worthless as Paco Hernandez should make trouble for the living. I have informed headquarters the body is to be removed quickly—in perhaps an hour. Examination of the parking lot can wait till morning. The official report will merely say that Paco was knifed in an alley near Figueroa Street."

He looked at me apologetically.

"We shall have to take away the station wagon, Major. I don't expect to find anything, but we'll have to check for Paco's fingerprints—perhaps others'." He looked at Timeo. "There's no need for you to stay any longer, Timeo. I have a few more questions for Major McKendrick. We'll let ourselves out."

"Thank you, Captain," said the restaurant owner. "Just snap the master light switch at the door and be certain the lock is on." He waved at the bar. "Help yourself, of course," and left.

In the silence of the empty room, we could hear the sound of his car starting up and leaving the parking lot. Halloran got himself a bottle of beer. He didn't bother with a glass but swigged it down out of the bottle. He stood in front of Hernandez.

"Questions, Captain?" he said gently. "It's been a long day for all of us."

Hernandez didn't hear him. His brow was furrowed with deep thought.

"Why was the car returned here?" he asked. "To warn

McKendrick they still had his wife and kids?" He answered his own question with a vigorous nod.

"On the surface, bringing back the car makes sense. It avoids the need for a telephone call to you that conceivably might be traced. They will know or suspect of course that there is a tap on your phone. But there must be more to it than that."

"What do you know that you haven't told us, Mc-Kendrick?" he said sharply.

"What makes you think I know anything?" I said irritably. "I told Sanders all I know, I told Logan, I told you."

Halloran shook his head. "No, Major, it's the only way it figures," he said. "Captain Hernandez thought all they wanted was the ring. By putting the ring in the hands of Papa Mendoza, by using Paco as the contact, he made it easy for them to get the ring. All they had to do was pay Papa off, give him a profit on the $5,500 he gave you. They had to come out in the open to do that. That's what the captain was counting on—a lead. But putting your car back here, even before they got the ring, that can mean only one thing. They want you to hear loud and clear that you got to stay clammed up—about something you know—even if you don't know you know it."

"How could they know I'd see the car?"

"Where were you going to meet Paco for the payoff?"

"The back lot, he said," I answered. I looked at Captain Hernandez; the sick feeling was coming back. I said slowly: "That means they'd set up Paco. They meant to kill him from the beginning."

Halloran nodded. "Looks like that. They wanted him quiet." He looked at my face and quickly poured me a brandy.

"Drink up, Major, and don't take it so hard. It wasn't your doing. Paco was playing in a tough league—way over his head."

Hernandez shoved his empty glass at Halloran and drummed his fingers on the bar.

"There must be something, McKendrick, something that

108

has escaped us. Tell me how you got that ring again."

I told him. It was standard practice. All the guys in the squadron were doing it, prodded by Anne and the girls on the base, who dreamed up the boutique, mostly because they couldn't get over the "fantastic" bargains in the Far East that they'd never see again once they were shipped back to the States.

Our base in Kyoto did some training, some routine patrols, but it was situated ideally for a continuous flow of those semiurgent medium-top-secret courier flights to most of the big cities in the Orient. We used to kid about the flights; somehow they always seemed to occur so that the men in the squadron got to spend a weekend in Thailand or India or Hong Kong or some such place. We got a lot of old hands flying in and out of the base, regular Air Force types, who had spent years in the Orient and had done their share of bargain hunting over the years.

Anne and the girls were forever pumping them for the names of dealers or wholesalers, and few of us ever took off for a top-secret mission or its fictional equivalent without a list of names of such dealers or wholesalers and a couple of hundred dollars in American cash to pick up samples of jewelry, lace and similar lightweight merchandise that would fit in the plane's pod. Nor did the planes return without a delegation of the girls who ran the boutique meeting them on arrival. For them it was Christmas every Sunday evening. I suppose it was an important break on what was an essentially dull base. Most of the girls who worked in the boutique were like Anne. They got first crack at the shiny new baubles and they kept most of their flier-husbands slightly broke.

The Cambodian jaunt from Kyoto, I told Hernandez, wasn't a bit different from a couple of dozen such buying trips I made to a couple of dozen places. I went at Anne's request to Ying Po & Company, a slightly above-average tourist trap, explained the problem to the tiny owner with the wispy chin whiskers and brought the boodle back to the girls in the boutique.

When Anne and the kids went back to the States and I went into training for the F-4s, she remembered Ying Po's merchandise. After a year in Vietnam, I got a week off for R&R. I couldn't afford the usual R&R routine back in Hawaii, nor could I afford to bring Anne out there for the precious few days of rest. I chose to take my time in Cambodia for the best of all possible reasons: I got free transportation because Pinky Prentice dropped in at Ubon, big and boisterous as ever.

He spent the night with me in Pnompenh and we wandered around the town. I remembered Ying Po and Anne's anniversary at the same time.

"Why did you remember it at that particular time?" Hernandez asked.

I smiled. "Old Ying Po was a student of modern merchandising. He served all his American customers tea followed by a Scotch chaser."

"So you bought the ring," said Hernandez, and I nodded.

"Did he push that particular piece of merchandise?" Hernandez asked.

I tried to think back. I couldn't really remember. I had awakened late with a king-sized hangover. I had an early lunch and a couple of drinks, got a cab and went to Ying Po's.

I tried to recapture the scene. He was replacing a tray when I came in, straightened up, put it back on the counter. He greeted me cordially, busied himself with the tea, added the bottle of Johnnie Walker. I remember seeing the ring in the tray, thinking briefly how it would go with Anne's strawberry blonde hair, and then discarding the notion because it looked too expensive.

I trifled with what he offered me; they were too gaudy, too crude, too non-Anne, but I had two Scotches, and with that for courage pointed to the ring with the green stone. I whistled when Ying Po told me it was seventy-three dollars American. I had intended to spend only about twenty-five or thirty. He handed me the ring and went into the back of the shop while I made up my mind. Then

I said: "The hell with it, it's only money," and bought it, feeling sentimental as hell.

"And that's it, Captain Hernandez," I said.

"Did Colonel Prentice go with you?" Halloran asked hopefully.

"Gosh, no. I guess you'd call Pinky the drinking man's flier. Even after I got back to the hotel, he was sacked out. I didn't even get a chance to thank him for the lift."

"You went directly back to Ubon?" asked Hernandez.

"Right; I caught a C-46. Frankly, paying the seventy-three dollars for the ring left me flat. That's why I was just as glad I didn't get to talk to Pinky. I would have borrowed money from him and stayed on."

Hernandez brooded a bit, then shook his head. "There's got to be something. Sleep on it, McKendrick. If you get a glimmer, let me know."

I got up from the bar. It seemed to me that Hernandez was missing the point of the whole problem.

"You mean, Captain, I'm supposed to cooperate to the fullest extent?"

He nodded.

"Well, Captain, isn't it supposed to be a two-way street? What about my wife and kids? Aren't they likely to be in your territory now? What are you doing about it?"

He looked at me with infinite patience, took his wallet out of his back pocket and thumbed out a few snapshots.

They were Polaroid pictures—family groups around a Christmas tree. I saw a pretty woman and three little children. Except for the brown tones in the color, they were just like the ones I had in my own wallet—pretty wife, three healthy children.

"I've got it in mind, Major," he said. There was weariness in his voice. "Right now, we've got a pickup order out on every informer in the city of Tampa. We're squeezing them for the tiniest lead."

"Papa Mendoza?"

He shrugged. "He's in a hole somewhere, Major. He'll come out when he's good and ready."

"What about Logan and the FBI?"

"If Congressman Hammond can't push them around or won't, what chance do you think a local cop has?"

I knew my question was dirty pool, but I was getting desperate.

"Have you got a line, Captain, on the informer in your department—the one who tipped off my meeting with you in the Hernandez grocery store?"

He turned his back on me and replaced the brandy bottle on the back bar. "It's time to go, Sergeant," he said. He waited till Halloran escorted me to my borrowed car; then he switched out the lights to Timeo's.

"If I were you, Major," Halloran said softly, "I'd sit quiet. This thing is turning messy; it's likely to get worse before it gets better."

"Not likely I'm going to do much with the FBI, the Air Force and now Captain Hernandez keeping tabs on me."

"Just as well," he said. "That way we know you're safe."

"Thanks loads, Sergeant," I said.

# 9

Halloran followed me home, rode my tail right into the driveway—and it was a comforting feeling. The house lights were blazing and he got out and trailed me onto the porch. I peered through the window in the front door. It was Logan, in the upholstered chair as usual, watching the TV set in the living room. Halloran looked into the room, patted me on the shoulder.

"See you, Major," he said.

I hung up my jacket without a word to Logan, put the knife on the coffee table. The sonofabitch was eating Mrs. Friendly's pie.

He switched off the TV and smiled amiably.

"Those Bogart movies really grab me," he said. "I got the coffee on, Major. Join me?"

I could have done without the company, but the coffee

sounded good. Like all the thin guys I have known, he dumped sugar into his cup like it was going out of style, stirred it slowly.

"I hear you been busy, Major," he said. "Hobnobbing with congressmen, getting your picture in the paper, pawning a ring, getting mixed up with a murder. I'd count that a full day for an amateur."

I sipped the coffee. "Did you also hear my car is back?" I asked quietly.

"Yes," he said. "That takes a lot of figuring. Seems like somebody's trying to tell you something."

"Captain Hernandez figures the return of the car is connected with the ring. He thinks there's something I know that someone doesn't want me telling."

"Do you know something, Major?" The smile had gone out of his voice.

I shook my head. "If I do, I can't remember it."

"I wish you'd think harder, Major. It's important."

"To me too," I said grimly. "I've got a wife and three kids at stake."

"That reminds me, Major," he said. "The word went out to the Bureau at ten thirty tonight. Unofficially, it's now listed as a 'suspected kidnaping.'"

"So Congressman Hammond does swing some weight?" I said with a touch of sarcasm.

"You mean that stupid picture in the paper tonight?" he asked bitingly. "Don't you believe it! I gave the order myself."

"Why?"

"It's simple," he said. "It's not likely that anyone as stupid as you are could be guilty of anything. Of course, that opinion is not shared by Colonel Sanders. When he heard that you were about to pawn the ring, which he regards as government property, he wanted you in the MacDill stockade pronto. 'A common criminal,' I think, was the kindest thing he said about you. By the way, how much money did you get for the ring?"

"Fifty-five hundred dollars," I said.

113

He whistled softly. "I guess the boys from Internal Revenue will be looking you up, unless the Customs boys get to you sooner."

"I'm not worried," I said. "What happens now that the case is listed as a 'suspected kidnaping'?"

"It's pretty much routine. Descriptions of your wife, children, go out to the bureaus. They go to local police stations, sheriffs, under the heading of 'believed missing.' We talked to your friend, Sam, from the highway, trying to get enough out of him to identify the man with the long hair he told you about."

"Sounds like a lot of busy work," I said. "When do you think you'll have something?"

"I could say soon, but forty-eight hours would be about right. The fact is we've really got only one thing worthwhile. We're pretty sure we're dealing with some part of the Fidelista movement."

"Christ, you ought to have a lot on that. You've been at it since the Bay of Pigs."

A look of disgust came over him. "Pigs, smigs," he said shortly. "That's a CIA operation and what the hell they're doing is more than anybody can figure out. We get nothing from the CIA and they get nothing from us. It's a hell of a way to run a government."

"I thought you guys got together, like you're working with Sanders now."

He snorted in scorn. "You know what the trouble with this country is, McKendrick? Every sonofabitch has a Jesus complex! He's got a plan to save the world. Maybe he could do it too, if he'd let the working stiffs like you and me in on it. I ask you only one question: How much did you know, really know about Air Force plans in Ubon?"

"Damn little."

"That's the way it goes, with us, only in spades. We've got a couple of hundred suspected Fidelistas in our raw files—that means gossip, rumor, things we run into in the course of other investigations. We could pinpoint the exact involvement of every one of these people in twenty-four hours if we had access to the CIA files. But that's not permitted under our system of national security, whatever the hell that means these days. So half the people in our files may be working for the CIA, may be working for the Fidelistas, may be double, triple, quadruple agents for all I know."

"Like you said, Logan, it's a hell of a way to run a government," I said sourly.

He got to his feet. "Do me a favor, McKendrick. Sit tight for forty-eight hours. Take up needlepoint or something. It's going to be tough enough without you mucking around."

"No promises, Logan," I said. I walked with him to the front door. He put his hand on the knob and turned back to me. He looked grave.

"McKendrick, I'm going to tell you something. It's for your own good. If it comes up, I'll deny that I ever mentioned it. Don't get too involved with Congressman Hammond. I can't tell you why, but he could be bad medicine."

"The raw file, again, Logan?" I asked cynically.

He nodded. "There's some reason to believe he's a bit of a swinger. And his boy, Bob Kelly, really gets around, some mighty strange people. Sure, I know that Hammond's a liberal and you get some mighty queer people in that barrel, but I'm talking about more than that."

"I wonder, Logan, what the raw file has on me?"

I was curious about that certainly, but I really asked the question to conceal from him how the information about Hammond shook me. For a moment, I even debated telling him I'd seen Kelly outside Papa Mendoza's house.

But Logan wasn't looking at me. He was squinting at the wall, refreshing his recollection. Then he recited mechanically: "B.A. Niagara University, 1957, ROTC four years. Pilot training on T-33, Lackland, with a rating of 3.9, assigned to Air Training Command, Craig for five years, same rating, special training in survival, author of a single paper, 'Bucketing and Other In-Flight Stresses,' *Air Force Journal,* March 1962, special citation, Office of Air Engineering, Wright Air Force Base, assigned to Kyoto for four years, assistant base commander, chief of flight training, returned to the U.S. January 1967 for retraining F-4s, MacDill Air Force Base, assigned as squadron commander Ubon, 81st Fighter Squadron, 152 missions, Air Medal with clusters, Presidential citation. Performance rating 3.9, squadron mortality rate 11.9."

It was quite a performance. "That all?"

"Not quite." He smiled. "Married Anne Sanderson, February, 1959, three children, Presbyterian, but nonchurchgoer, no drinker, indifferent golfer and you subscribe to *The New York Times* and the History Book of the Month Club. One thing more: you had, one month ago, a bank balance of $213.54 and outstanding current debits of something over $400."

"You convinced me of two things, Logan," I said with a slight smile. "You do a pretty good job of investigating and I'm tired as hell."

There was an echoing emptiness as I went round the house, putting out the lights, locking the front and back doors. From the mess in the kitchen, I could see that Logan was a bachelor. I made a final check of the ashtrays and went into the bedroom.

The empty echo changed to an aching silence as I saw Anne's bed, made in unaccustomed neatness. I couldn't help myself. I left the bedroom and wandered into the children's rooms. The maid had picked the clothes and toys off the floor, put them away neatly. But I wasn't thinking that hard about them now; my mind was busy with something Logan had said—or hadn't said. Something in my mind; a tiny little relay in the back of my mind was struggling to close a circuit. It was important—but I was getting a faint message that it had to do with me, not my family.

One of my fitness reports had said: "McKendrick is reflexive, rather than reflective." It was a little too literary-precious for the formalized Air Force reports, but it wasn't a bad description of a fighter pilot who's still alive. I don't have all that talent for intense analysis of problems of logic. I'm the kind of guy who sleeps on a problem and a lot of times the answer is there with the morning orange juice.

I pushed the mess back in my mind and got into bed. I wish I could say that I tossed and turned in worry, but I dropped right off. Training, I guess.

It wasn't the best of all possible dreams, but then it never is. I was back over Min Da, and the same lick of flame had appeared on the leading edge of the right wing, and the red and green tracer fragments were dancing on top of the canopy.

I kept thinking frantically, "I've got to get out," and at the same time, the other part of my mind kept looking down at the jungle and saying, "Jesus, it's dark down there!" I tugged at the ejection handle between my legs and nothing happened and then I reached out in front of my face for the Jesus handle—the reserve ejection system that takes out the canopy. As always in the dream, the oxygen mask was choking me—and I woke up, but I still couldn't breathe. I realized all of a sudden that it wasn't the oxygen mask of my dreams. I was awake and there was a huge hand across my mouth, and an immense weight was across my body, smothering every effort I made to writhe loose.

A voice was saying softly over and over again: "Quiet, Major. It's Papa Mendoza." It took a moment for the quiet voice to pierce my panic and then I stopped struggling. The hand left my mouth and I felt the weight slide off my body. In the dark, I saw the hulking shadow of Philippe. Mendoza was sitting alongside my bed. He had a tiny flashlight cupped in his hand, the beam directed at the floor. I could feel the heavy sweat on my forehead and I reached for the night light. Mendoza gripped my arm.

"I'd leave it off, Major," he said, "till we talk."

I wanted a cigarette badly.

"We have located your wife and children, Major," he said, and I sat bolt upright.

"Where?"

"In a warehouse, close to the *barrio*," he said.

"Have you told the FBI—Hernandez?" I asked.

There was a slight pause. "No, that is not possible," he said.

"What the hell do you mean it is not possible?" I whispered angrily.

"The man in the office, whose attack on my life you so fortunately diverted, was very difficult. He gave us the necessary information, but he was very stubborn. I'm afraid that the arrangements for the disposal of the body must be made very delicately. I should not like him to be linked to me. It would be very bad for business. It would prove very embarrassing if the man were to come to the attention of Captain Hernandez or the government."

"What do we do, then?

"We take them out," he said simply. "I thought you would be interested in accompanying us."

It took me all of five seconds to decide. I climbed out of my bed and started to slip into my trousers. Philippe put his hand on my shoulder.

"Something dark if you will, Major." I dropped the pants and went to the closet. Slipping into the familiar flight suit, I felt some of the stomach-knotting tenseness that I had felt almost daily in Ubon for the last thirteen months. There's some fear in it, but there's a lift of excitement too, knowing the mission has been set and there's no turning back. I laced the heavy boots up swiftly, took the insignia off the flight cap, removed my lapel badge and said: "Let's go."

They moved out the back door, like a pair of veteran alley cats, with precision, through the moments of frozen inaction and then the sudden stealthy scurry to cover. We slipped through the back lots of two streets of houses. Philippe nudged my arm and pointed to a black panel truck standing next to a large hedge.

He drove slowly, heading away from my street and the watching FBI men. We made a wide circle of the city, then headed downtown on side streets to the *barrio*. We had not quite reached the warehouse section when Philippe turned into a dark alley and let the truck come to a halt. We climbed out and I followed them through a door. It was an auto-body repair shop and the cannibalized cars and the dim lights gave me a funereal feeling.

"Evening, Major," said Halloran, stepping out from behind a black Chevrolet. He was dressed as I was in the dark green flight suit, boots and cap.

"What are you doing here?" I asked.

"Just helping out, Major. Papa gave me a call, said he needed a hand. Here I am."

Only then did I notice he had his service automatic, stuck in the calf pocket of his right leg, the way we carry them on routine flights. He reached into his hip pocket and handed me another. "Just in case, Major." I took the gun, automatically checked the action and slipped it into my own leg pocket.

I looked at his bland face. I had difficulty clearing my throat. A lump had suddenly come up there.

"You don't have to do this, Sergeant," I said.

He looked pointedly at Mendoza and Philippe. "You're wrong there, Major," he said. "Anne and the kids are Air Force too. We take care of our own." He grinned suddenly at me, reached down and wiped his hands on the greasy floor. With two swift motions, he smeared both sides of my face.

"If you'll pardon me, Major, you're missing some of our natural talents for night combat." Both Papa Mendoza and Philippe smiled at the joke. Papa motioned us to follow him.

It was a tiny cubicle of an office, complete with desk, chair, an adding machine and a dusty phone. The shelves were lined with boxes of fan belts, spark plugs and similar accessories. Philippe cleaned off the desk and disappeared into the outer workroom. He returned with a set of blueprints under his arm, a tray with a coffeepot and four elegant demitasse cups.

"Unless you prefer brandy, Major," said Papa Mendoza, looking up from pouring the coffee.

"Not before flying, thank you," I said automatically. I laughed with him.

"Excellent," he said. "Philippe?"

Philippe spread the blueprints on the desk. In the upper left-hand corner, in architectural lettering, were the words: "Warehouse, No. 4, Utopia Corporation."

Papa Mendoza said: "About the plans, Major. I dabble in real estate. The building is owned by an old friend, Manny Epstein. He let me have them so I could determine if the building is a suitable investment."

"At three in the morning?" I asked.

"When else?" Mendoza said politely. "Manny runs the most successful gambling house in town."

Philippe pointed a large black finger at a portion of the plan. "The children and your wife are here, Major. It is a small section at the back of the warehouse, on the fifth floor. It was formerly the apartment of an owner of the warehouse."

"Not at all uncomfortable, Major," added Papa Mendoza. "The former owner had interesting hobbies—which may be why Manny Epstein owns it now."

Philippe waited patiently, much as sergeants all through history have endured the irrelevant witticisms of commanding officers.

He satisfied himself that Mendoza had nothing more to say and turned to Halloran.

"There are five men. One is here"—he pointed to the first-floor plan—"commanding the elevator and the stairs. Another on the fifth floor at the head of the elevators. He carries an automatic rifle. I believe it is an M-16. The remainder are stationed at this door, the door of the apartment on the fifth floor. They check in the apartment, in succession, one at a time, at fifteen-minute intervals. They are well trained, disciplined. They go, as you say, Sergeant, by the book."

I felt a moment's misgivings. "But that means, even if we knock out the first three, one more is bound to be with Anne and the kids."

Halloran and Philippe exchanged glances.

"No, Major," said Halloran quietly. "Philippe says they go by the book. When an officer says 'by the book' he means it. When an enlisted man says he's going by the book, he means it, but he means he's always got another witness to prove he did if something happens. What Philippe has been saying is that every fifteen minutes, the man who goes in and out of the apartment is going to be checking with the outside man outside, making sure the outside man knows he is doing his job every fifteen minutes on the nose."

Philippe had the look of a man who is finally understood in his own language, even if it is a foreigner who understands him.

"There are always three of them in the room outside the apartment every fifteen minutes and one man by the elevator," said Mendoza.

"Right, Papa," said Philippe.

"Then there is no problem," Mendoza said briskly. "We have four guns—one for each."

I guess the military trained me badly, but I couldn't believe what I had heard.

"You mean, we each, each one of us, for Christ's sake, kill one and that's it? We don't ask them to surrender? Just blast. My God, that's murder in cold blood."

"You may leave now, Major, if you wish," Mendoza said coldly.

I didn't like that. "But cold blood, for God's sake?"

Halloran and Philippe looked at each other. They deferred to Mendoza.

"Major," he said after searching my face, "I invited you along on this event because I am grateful to you for saving my life, and because I felt that each man must prove his *machismo*—manhood. To this degree, perhaps I was sentimental. But I must tell you this is a matter of business as well. These animals not only seized your wife and children, but they attempted to invade my territory, attack me in person."

His chin was rigid with indignation.

121

"They have attacked me, Major."

"In cold blood, Papa," I said stubbornly.

He threw out his hands in despair. The colonel who taught me the trigonometry of rocket fire often wore the same expression. I was a dull and probably invincibly ignorant pupil.

Mendoza looked at his watch. "We shall leave here in a half-hour, Major. You may come with us or stay, as you like. But if I may, I shall take a few of our remaining minutes to improve your knowledge of your own profession. You are a professional military man. That is good, it is an honorable profession.

"We fight tonight people who are guerrillas. This is a word that is fashionable with your editorial writers who, as they did so disastrously with Fidel Castro, envision a ragged band of freedom fighters sallying bravely forth to defend the people.

"It is possible that there may have been a time in history when there were such dedicated men. But they soon lose that dedication. Their aim quickly becomes the right aim and the only aim. But in a very short time, they become perverted by the violence they themselves practice. Violence becomes an art and a profession—the perfection of the profession is killing.

"I should think that would be clear to you. You have seen at first hand how the North Vietnamese fight war. It is killing, pure and simple. There are subtle variations of the killing, and that kind of killing is most highly prized which is unexpected, undignified and horrifying. For the end purpose of the guerrilla, whether he be Mau Mau, North Vietnamese, Fidelista or American Woodsman, is terror.

"Che Guevara, whom your college students adore, was a bad guerrilla. He did not truly understand that when the terror succeeds in its object of toppling the establishment, you now become the establishment, and the kind of terror that was successful in the early days must be changed. That is why Fidel sent him to play with his machine guns and plastic explosives in other countries.

"You conceive of this mission tonight as some kind of a good-guys-versus-bad-guys movie script. It is not so, Major. We go to rescue your wife and children because these terrorists have invaded my territory. I am the establishment. It is good, will be good when we take your wife and children from these men. It will teach them that Mendoza is not to be trifled with. They cannot invade my territory, kill my policeman, stab my agent, Paco, without severe punishment. That is truly the reason I cannot permit Captain Hernandez or the FBI to join us. They would bring these men to trial. That is unnecessary. I have tried them, found them guilty and sentenced them to death. Now, Philippe, let us examine the map."

He turned away from me with icy disdain.

It wasn't a very subtle plan—maybe the good ones aren't. Most of my fighting is done from one to three miles from my adversary. Perhaps that's why they ignored me completely, even Halloran, but talked together in low voices. Mendoza made one telephone call in a quiet voice. He turned to the other two, said with satisfaction: "The sergeant is right. Manny says fully protected, even the top floor with the apartment."

We moved out then into the black panel truck. There was no conversation save Mendoza's curt comment to me: "You will remain in the rear at all times, Major. In accordance with your principles, you will shoot only in direct emergencies."

I resented the comment but sensibly kept my mouth shut. I was watching the street signs, the ones that still had some illumination, where the local kids hadn't knocked out the bulbs on the streetlamps. I knew we were getting closer and closer to the warehouse district, near the docks in the bay.

We made a right turn and slid quietly down a street, both sides of which were lined with soot-covered red brick buildings. Halloran jabbed me sharply in the ribs. "On the right, Major." I took a quick look, thought I could see a sign: "Warehouse 4," but I couldn't be sure. There was nothing to distinguish it from all the others—some windows boarded up, the remainder black and faceless, and on the right-hand side of the building front the sign: "Shaftway," which undoubtedly harbored the elevator. It had a huge steel roll-up door to the loading bay which looked tightly locked. So did the heavily battened wooden door, with the tiny office, near the shaftway.

We drove sedately down the street, for all the world like any one of the hundreds of bakery and other food trucks making predawn deliveries throughout the city.

We turned right again at the corner, went on for two blocks and parked midway in the third, at the farthest point from the streetlight. A slight figure darted from a dark doorway to the truck and scrambled into the driver's seat alongside Philippe.

"*Buenos días,* Guillermo," said Mendoza.

"*Buenos días,* Papa, Philippe." At the sound of the high treble voice, I leaned forward. The boy could not have been more than ten.

"May I have a cigarette, Papa, please?" said the boy.

"It is a filthy habit, Guillermo, as you have heard on television many times. It is bad for your health and will lead you to an early end," Mendoza said severely.

"*Por favor,*" persisted the boy.

"The young!" Mendoza said despairingly. "They learn nothing. Well, this once. Philippe, give him one, only one."

Papa Mendoza should have saved his breath. The boy was an accomplished street smoker; the light in the cupped hands, the noisy exhalation of the first drag, and the carefully concealed cigarette in a downturned palm revealed he was an old hand at avoiding adult surveillance. I could only hope that he hadn't hit the grass trail yet, but even that was unlikely in this neighborhood.

"Guillermo," said Mendoza, "I am told that you are a close observer of this neighborhood."

"True," said the boy, the grin on his face showing in the dashboard light.

"It is said also that you have access to all the warehouses —access that is not of general knowledge."

"True."

"You perhaps are familiar with Warehouse Number 4 on Poinsettia?"

There was a touch of hesitation before the boy replied.

"Yes, but—"

"But what, Guillermo?"

"There are men presently in Warehouse Number 4. They are"—he was groping for a word—"they are bad, very bad. It is not safe in Warehouse 4 at this moment. Besides, there is very little of value there."

"Thank you for telling me of the men, Guillermo," Mendoza said. "It is because of them that we are here. They are"—he turned to Halloran—"what is the word in American, Sergeant?"

"Squatters?" suggested Halloran.

"Precisely," said Mendoza. "They are squatters; what is more, they are not of the neighborhood. It is important to my friend Manny Epstein that they be removed."

"That is good," said the boy seriously. "It is not good that men from outside make it impossible for those in the neighborhood to visit their own places. But if you are to go in, it is necessary that I do not merely tell you how, but that I show you."

"It may be dangerous, Guillermo," said Mendoza.

"Of course it is dangerous," said Guillermo. "The one by the elevator and the stairs has a gun. I have seen this myself. That is why it is better that I take you myself."

Guillermo had the assurance of a vacuum cleaner salesman. He directed the parking of the truck and led out the four of us like a platoon leader in the rice paddies. We hugged the wall at his hand signals, plunged through alleys, over fences and wound up behind the building next to Warehouse 4. He gave a hand signal to Halloran, who gave him a stirrup boost and a heave to a boarded windowsill, ten feet above our heads. I saw the flash of a knife in the half-light, heard a creak, and the boards on the window came away as easily as if they were fastened to the frame with nothing more substantial than whipped margarine.

I looked up at the windowsill and wondered how the last of the four of us was going to make it. Another creak solved my problem. Guillermo appeared suddenly from a street-level door that looked as if it hadn't been opened in years. But it moved smoothly on quietly oiled hinges, indicating that Guillermo and his friends had used it often.

Lighting our way with a candle stuck in a beer bottle, Guillermo led us up two flights of stairs. Holding the candle behind his back, he brought us over to a tightly iron-shuttered window. The heavy shutters were greased too. They swung back without so much as a creak. I crowded to the window with the others. Warehouse 4 was only thirty feet away, but so far as I could see, there was no way across.

Guillermo looked at our bewildered faces.

"The tie rod," he said with a grin, pointing directly down from the windowsill. It was a long slender steel rod thrust through the single exterior wall of Warehouse 3 and Warehouse 4, and anchored on the walls where Warehouse 3, butted on that of 2, and where Warehouse 4 butted on that of Warehouse 5. Such rods were vitally necessary in the buildings of this old section, which rested on the ancient shores of the bay, since pushed back by man's greed and ingenuity.

"*Madre de Dios!*" Mendoza said. I could see what he meant. The tie rod was a good six feet below the windowsill.

"*No es nada,*" said Guillermo, after a look at our faces. He disappeared somewhere in the bowels of the warehouse. He returned in a matter of minutes. The package of clothesline he carried still bore the imprint of the local discount store from which Guillermo's busy men had undoubtedly pilfered it. I wondered for just a fraction of a second what the Boy Scouts could teach Guillermo.

He raised the window quietly, crouched for a second on the sill and without a backward look, hung by his fingertips and dropped to the rod. He teetered perilously for a moment, squatted and grabbed the rod with two hands. Then he straightened up carefully to his full height. As deftly as a circus wire-walker, he slipped across the tie rod in sneakered feet, reached up and slipped out of sight through a window in Warehouse 4.

Only then did I see what the clothesline was for. Guillermo had trailed it behind him. Halloran had fastened it to a post on our side and the boy now tied up his end in Warehouse 4. I looked at the thin white strand as doubtfully as Papa Mendoza, but Philippe seemed totally assured. He let himself down on the tie rod and foot by foot, one hand on the line, maneuvered his way across.

He didn't climb to the windowsill, however, but bracing himself against the wall, hauled on the line till it was taut.

I held Mendoza's wrist as he clung to the sill, reaching down for the tie rod. He was a couple of inches short.

"Let go with your hands," I whispered. "I can hold you."

His strained and sweating face was alongside mine. "I am a fool, Major," he said. "But when there is no one else to trust, one must put one's faith in the devil." He closed his eyes, let his hands go free and dropped. For a moment I thought I had lost him. He swayed back and forth like a wobbly top. I drove my free shoulder against the window frame and steadied him. Gasping for breath, he finally caught the rope with one hand, straddled the tie rod and painfully inched his way across.

Philippe heaved him like a bag of oats to the sill of the window in Warehouse 4 and he scuttled inside like a specially awkward sand crab. Halloran made the trip so easily that I felt totally confident of my own ability. It wasn't any more exhausting than a week of survival exercise. Philippe apparently didn't feel I was anywhere near as valuable as Papa Mendoza. He'd disappeared from the end of the tie rod when I got there, but Halloran's great black hands hauled me in with no ceremony and less dignity.

Papa Mendoza still sat on the floor, exhaling great breaths of air. "Mother of God!" he wheezed. "To be doing this at my time of life. It's undignified." He put out a hand and Halloran helped him to his feet. He reached over and took Guillermo by the shoulder. He pointed to the window. "*Muchas gracias.* Out!"

The boy's face fell. "I should very much like to stay, Papa Mendoza. It may one day be useful to learn how to remove squatters."

"In good time, you will learn," said Mendoza. "Of that I am certain. But there is always tomorrow."

He took out a roll of bills and in the light of his pencil flashlight carefully selected a twenty-dollar bill.

"Now go," said Mendoza. The boy pocketed the bill, straddled the windowsill and stopped suddenly.

"Papa Mendoza?" he hissed.

"Yes?"

"There is the matter of the clothesline," the boy said politely.

"So there is," Mendoza whispered. He took two single bills out of his pocket and gave them to the boy. "*Vaya con Dios*," he said. The boy's head disappeared in the dark. Mendoza waited till the boy had climbed into the window opposite, then turned to us and said thoughtfully: "An excellent businessman, Guillermo. I must keep in touch with him."

I got close to Halloran's ear. "Now what?" I asked.

"No sweat, Major," he said softly. "That one down there" —he pointed—"he's there to make sure no one comes up. Down, he ain't expecting." He sat on the floor pulling me down with him. He unlaced his boots and motioned me to do the same.

He beckoned me close to him. "Philippe will lead out. I'll follow him six steps behind. You cover me from the same distance."

I nodded at Papa Mendoza and he shook his head.

"No. Someone's got to cover and if we have any trouble downstairs, we'll have to move fast."

We huddled at the top of the stairs. Halloran gave Philippe the go signal with a gentle pat on the shoulder. With every step down that Philippe's bare black feet took him, I could feel the excitement rise; I had to swallow continually to clear my throat and I couldn't lick the dryness from my lips. Halloran's hand covering my own shocked me on contact. "The safety," he reminded me. I snapped it off, counted the successive lowering of Halloran's head on the steps below me. I should have waited till he was six steps ahead; I stepped off on the fifth from sheer nervousness and felt the shock of the cold railing on my left hand.

We met on the landing halfway down and listened. The only sound was the soft driving beat of a Latin American band.

"Bastard's got the radio on," Halloran breathed. "Better and better." He pointed and Philippe moved down. I was glad I wasn't the only one nervous. Halloran, just as I had before, moved out on the count of five instead of six. I don't know what I expected, but I stayed poised six steps down from the landing and I heard nothing—nothing except a small sound like a native woman pounding a piece of wet wash against a rock. I counted fifty to myself and couldn't stand it any longer. I moved cautiously down the steps, slid to the left on the last and burst into the reception room with the gun shoved ahead of me. Halloran was standing with his huge silhouette framed in the light. Philippe was beyond him, bending over.

In a moment I knew I'd never again have the dream of Min Da with the red and green fragments dancing on the canopy, the rapid flashes of the guns and the deep darkness of the valley pregnant with death.

I'll dream of those thirteen dark steps and what lay in the light beyond when Halloran turned slowly to me and took a step to the side and I saw what Philippe was bending over. The man in the swivel chair was tipped way back. His chin seemed to be resting on the bright steel that had been driven into his throat. The underside of his chin had a bright splash of blood like an obscene scar; the rest had cascaded down the front of his white sports shirt, down his hand and onto the comic book he had been holding.

I spun, ready to throw up, when Halloran sprang to my side. He locked his huge arm around by chest, held my nose firmly between two huge fingers.

"Not now, goddamn it, Major; we ain't got time." I

struggled for breath for only a moment, then held up my hand for him to stop.

"Okay, Sergeant," I said, "I think I can handle it now."

"We couldn't take a chance that he'd get off a quick shot. Philippe got him with a throwing knife." He looked at me sympathetically. "It ain't pretty, Major, but then neither is napalm."

He beckoned Philippe and they came together and compared watches. Then he pulled me to the corner farthest away from the stairs.

"Here's the way it's going to be, Major," he said softly. "In about five minutes, one of them's going to be inspecting the apartment and your wife and kids. There's bound to be a certain amount of moving around, so we'll have cover. In exactly ten minutes, you'll move out of here. Move to the fourth floor. Wait there exactly four minutes, then move to the fifth floor. In one minute, all hell will break loose. Now, Major, hear me and hear me clear. Don't move from the doorway at the head of those stairs until exactly sixty seconds after you arrive at the fifth floor. Now, if you'll repeat."

He cocked his ear toward me and listened carefully. "That's got it, Major."

He started to climb to his feet, but I caught his arm.

"Anne and the kids—how can I be sure they'll be safe?"

"You can't, Major, but then they're not safe now. I can promise you only one thing. Any sonofabitch in that room outside the apartment has got to go through me, and I mean through me, to get near them when we move in. If I were you, I'd hang in there easy."

He patted his waist. I couldn't tell what he had under the flight suit, but there was a marked bulge around his belt line. "I got us a little old diversion here."

"What is it?"

"Not saying a word"—he smiled—"otherwise it wouldn't be a diversion. I got an idea it will surprise you too."

He got to his feet, crushed my wrist in a huge hand.

"Major, mind what I told you. The fifth floor and sixty seconds."

# 10

Philippe hadn't said a word. He watched Halloran leave me and head for the stairs. I saw him start to follow; then he stopped, looked around the room. He went to one of the corners, found a drop cloth that was apparently a relic from a long-gone paint job. He draped the paint cloth over the dead man. I thought it was a tribute to my sensitive stomach till he said: "Maybe you'd better sit behind the door, Major. Someone might show up."

It was a hard ten minutes. I turned off the Latin American rock 'n' roll or whatever the hell it was. I've never believed in the Good Neighbor Policy strongly enough to include their music. I don't care if it's called the conga, the samba or anything else. It's the kind of music that I think will someday go higher into a special kind of chromatic scale, get more intense or whatever it takes to trigger their minds —and then we'll have a violence the like of which we've never seen.

In the wearisome ten-minute stretch I took my courage in my hand and went through the man's pockets. He had a few dollars and a picture of himself grinning toothily at a broad-beamed blonde. I thought for a moment I might be able to identify the beach background, but it was like the beaches the world over. He also had a St. Christopher's medal in his pocket. I had the feeling that now that he was dead, he still might have need of a guide.

I made only one change in the pattern ordered by Sergeant Halloran. I stopped for a few seconds on the second floor to pick up my boots. I didn't know what was going to happen, but I didn't fancy myself getting far on the streets of Tampa in stocking feet. I hung them round my neck with the laces knotted. I had never fancied a barefoot world.

I took the stairs one at a time, pausing at first to listen for sounds ahead of me. After a few pauses, when I heard nothing, I was a little less attentive. I began to think, surprisingly, of the last quarrel Anne and I had had. It was about her habit of walking and working about the house without shoes or slippers. Like most of our quarrels, this one had no special point. She'd been raised in Florida and spent most of her life without shoes. Going barefoot was as natural to her as it was to wake up in the morning with a smile of delighted wonder that the world and the people she loved were still with her.

It was as senseless as most married quarrels. But she and our three redheaded children donned shoes, slippers and sneakers for three whole days. They also wore a look that indicated they were doing their utmost to satisfy the whims of a thoughtless and unloving tyrant.

The regret I felt for that quarrel took me to the fourth floor and I checked my watch. The mystery stories that I read incessantly say old houses creak in the dark. Old warehouses don't. They are stiller than the grave—a stillness of the abandoned, the irretrievable.

I glanced at the sticky second-hand on my watch, going through the universal routine of the impatient traveler, giving it vigorous and frequent shakes. Finally I kept repeating the nonsense of that old proverb: A watched pot never boils. I found this so intriguing that I started switching it around. A boiled pot is never watched, which seemed to me in those interminable moments to have a universal wisdom of its own. For one nonsensical moment, I debated with myself if I shouldn't lie down on the floor and take a nap—as I have many times I've had to wait in the Air Force.

The second hand released me from the squirrel cage and I crept up the next flight of steps to the fifth floor. It was headed by a battleship gray door that said, "Manager" and, in lower-case letters, "authorized personnel only."

I moved closer to the door, stealthily grasped the doorknob. As carefully as I could, I laid my ear against the door. All I could hear was more goddamned Latin American music.

Then I made an interesting discovery. In order to grasp the doorknob, I had shifted the gun to my left hand. I realized that all I knew about breaking into a room was what I had seen in the movies. I stepped back to survey the situation. The procedure was awkward as hell, but the only way I could figure to manage the job was to grab the knob in my left hand, turn it at the appropriate moment, shove the door forward and rush in, my gun in the right hand.

I carefully slid my feet over to the left-hand side of the door about three feet away from the doorknob. I felt a sudden cold trickle on the back of my neck, but disregarded it. I thought it was a bead of sweaty fear. But the drops came faster and I turned slowly to discover the source. In the next moment, I got a face full of water. In my suddenly sopping stocking feet, I stepped aside and looked for the source of the water. Overhead the sprinkler valve was turning with slow precision, showering water down on me and the surrounding area. I grinned at Sergeant Halloran's diversion, a blow torch to the sprinkler system.

From behind the door, I heard a hoarse bellow of rage drown out the radio, joined in a moment by other howls. I grabbed the knob, turned it, shoved as hard as I could and rushed in. Before the door was even half-open, I heard the repeated thunderous bursts of the guns. It was like a scene from a bad movie—Halloran prone on the floor, the great left elbow supporting the gun hand, peering through the smoke. Philippe had come through the back door of the manager's office. He was holding his gun steadily enough, but he was rubbing the left side of his head and glaring at the oak desk that he had plunged into. Papa Mendoza was crouched in the wide-open door behind him, gun in hand. His head was moving like that of a bantam rooster in the barnyard, quick, anxious, checking the four men on the floor. They'd caught them in a bunch—even the one guarding the elevator, who rushed in when the sprinkler started. It wasn't pretty; most close-range slaughter with a forty-five isn't. Now they lay in a deadly sprawl, the blood from the gaping holes thinned in its trickling by the water that still poured from the spinning wheels on the ceiling pipes.

"Anne? The kids?" I asked.

"Back there," said Halloran, waving his left hand.

I turned in the direction he'd indicated, took a step forward. The door burst open, a blur of a figure shot through the opening. I caught the blue of the gun barrel and the hot red of the exploding muzzle at merging instants and then something smashed into my chest. It was like a giant trap closing on my chest, squeezing my heart and my lungs in the same terrible instant.

As I fell over backward, I heard only the blasphemy: "Jesus—to come this far," and the room blacked out.

Perhaps it was only one minute, perhaps two, perhaps five that I lay there, but it was a strange way to wake up. My eyes were open, but I had to be dreaming. I could feel the wet clothes on me, but my wife seemed to be mopping my face with a wet washcloth. It had to be Anne, my wife —nobody else had that incredible pink hair, nobody that ridiculous vocabulary of love. "McKendrick, McKendrick, you stupid, stupid, lovely man. Wake up!" It hurt like hell to move, but I got a hand across her back finally and squeezed her.

Even over the muffled sound of her sobs, I knew the rest of my family was in the room. I heard Shane, the youngest, saying: "Well, if he isn't drunk or dead, what's he doing lying on the floor?" I heard the rumble of Halloran's reply and I had a moment's sympathy for him. Shane takes after my side of the family. They argue long after common sense dictates a flag of surrender. Philippe was having his troubles with Mary, our gangly oldest and Sean, the middle redhead. From behind Anne, I could hear them arguing that they wanted a closer look at the dead men. "They're dead, anyway," Mary was saying. "Why can't we look at them?" As gently as I could, I pushed Anne aside.

"Knock it off," I bellowed. "Everybody out."

The rapid-fire "yes sirs" told me nothing had changed in the year I'd been away. Halloran shooed them out of the door, then pulled Anne to her feet.

"If you'll watch the children for a moment, ma'am?" he asked.

She looked down at me with brooding eyes.

"He'll be all right?"

"Sure thing," he said. She turned and left and he reached down and as if I were no more than a two-pound bag of dog meal, he pulled me to my feet. I staggered over to the corner of the oak desk and sat on it. The chest hurt like hell.

"What happened?" I asked.

He was shaking his head back and forth in wonder. Then he reached down to the floor and handed me my flying boots. The heel of the left boot was scarred and gouged as if a power saw had gone berserk.

"You sure got something going for you, Major," he said. "That slug would have gone clean through your chest. Instead it hit the heel of that boot and ricocheted off." He pointed to an ugly gash high up on the left of the door I'd come through.

I unzipped the front of my soggy flight suit. There was a massive bruise, just below my left nipple where the edge of the heel had smashed into it. I felt a moment's giddiness at the thought of the bullet, then a feeling of exhilaration and relief, precisely like the feelings I had whenever the mission broke off and we headed the F-4s home.

"Who was he? I thought Papa said there were only four of them." I didn't really care. I was just covering with words the silent prayer that kept going through my mind.

Halloran's nose wrinkled in disgust. He reached behind me, took a wallet from the oak desk and flipped it open. The police lieutenant's badge stared back at me.

"Frank Rivera, Captain Hernandez' assistant. He's the guy supposed to keep other cops clean."

"Then he's the one who tipped them off that I was coming to see you and Captain Hernandez?"

"It figures," said Halloran.

"How come he was here? Did he know we were coming?"

"I doubt it," said Halloran. "I think it was just one of those things. He dropped in to check up—something like that."

There was a strangeness in the room that I couldn't understand. Halloran looked up and I realized what it was. The water had stopped pouring from the ceiling.

"By the way, Sergeant," I said, "thanks for the diversion."

"No trouble at all, Major," he said, smiling. He showed me the blow torch on the desk. "I thought it worked out real fine."

Papa Mendoza came back into the room. He looked at the body of Rivera with distaste.

"It is always the way. Man proposes and God disposes. I do not think Captain Hernandez will be pleased at this most unlucky event."

"You better believe it," Halloran said lugubriously.

"Hell, he came out shooting," I said. "You had no choice."

Papa Mendoza looked at me like I was a very dull scholar indeed.

"You do not understand the complexity of the problem, Major," he said. "It will be most unpleasant for Captain Hernandez to learn that Frank Rivera has been disloyal to him and the department. But he will get over that."

He gestured contemptuously at the body on the floor. "That one is not the first policeman to be dishonest, nor will he be the last. But there is something more important than that to Hernandez. It is his image with his people. He has worked long and hard to persuade his people that Spanish-speaking people can make it on the force. He will not relish the publicity indicating that one of his men has gone sour."

I could sympathize with Hernandez' community-relations problem, but my chest was hurting like hell and I felt like I was getting a cold in the wet clothes and I wanted to get Anne and the kids home. They'd been through a lot, too.

"It will work out, I'm sure," I said. "Right now, I want to get home with my wife and my kids."

Mendoza looked startled. "But they are already gone, Major. I thought you knew."

"Gone?" I said in shock. "Where the hell to?"

He beckoned me with a finger, walked over to the sprawl of dead men on the floor. Methodically he turned each over.

"Do you recognize them, Major?" he asked.

I didn't and I shook my head.

"Exactly," he said, "they are nothings. Punks. Therefore, we have a problem."

"We?"

"We," he said firmly. "It is most unfortunate. But El Rojo is not included among our victims."

"How do you know El Rojo isn't one of these?" I asked suspiciously. I had the feeling I was being roped in even more tightly.

"It cost a good deal of money to get the information that these men were holding your wife and children here," he said.

"You got it out of the man in your office," I protested.

"It cost a good deal to dispose of him," he said coldly. "But in addition to your information, I got something that was even more valuable—a description of El Rojo."

"None of these fit that description?"

"Is any one of them redheaded?" he asked.

"You mean El Rojo is redheaded? A redheaded Cuban?" I suddenly remembered. "But I asked you before if El Rojo was redheaded."

He avoided that.

"El Rojo is half Cuban," he said. "His father was an American Army sergeant; his mother Cuban. He is needless to say a bastard. This may account in part for his violence."

"Where is he?"

"Who knows?" he said. "But that is why I took the liberty of having Philippe take your wife and children to a safe hiding place. I fear he will be very angry when he hears of our activity."

He made a lot of sense and I felt the same old feeling of depression come over me. No matter how I twisted, the net seemed to grow tighter around me. I had no feeling that El Rojo was going to throw in his hand.

"So what do we do now?" I asked.

"First," he said, "we make the present situation more palatable to Captain Hernandez." He held out his hand and Halloran reluctantly handed over his gun. Mendoza pried open Rivera's fingers, removed the forty-five and placed Halloran's gun in the man's palm and fingers. He took Rivera's hand and squeezed it around the butt and then let it drop an inch or two away from his fingertips.

"You don't really think Hernandez is going to buy that story, do you?" I asked skeptically. "That Rivera took on the four of them alone and got killed at the last minute?"

"Of course not," he said. "The story will be that Rivera joined you and Sergeant Halloran because of his anger at the death of one of his fellow policemen. Captain Hernandez will not believe that story either. But unless he is less wily than he was last week, I believe he will quickly point out that you and Sergeant Halloran cannot afford to get the Air Force tied into the four killings. I believe he will suggest to you that it will be wiser to tell the newspapers that Rivera did in fact turn the trick singlehandedly."

It sounded deviously Latin, but it would certainly give Hernandez what he wanted—the chance to get the department off clean. It would solve Hernandez' problem, but it didn't do a thing for mine.

I got up abruptly from the corner of the desk and put my shoes on. The heel seemed to walk all right.

"What now, Major?" asked Mendoza.

"I'm going to get something to cover these people up. They're beginning to depress me."

I went through the back door of the office, flipped on the overhead lights and began to look around. Even my squishy boots had a hollow sound in the cavernous emptiness of the warehouse. So far as I could see there was nothing at all in the huge room. Then against one of the far walls I made out the shape of a large square mound that seemed in the uncertain light to be covered with canvas. Now that the sprinklers were turned off, I didn't think the management would mind my borrowing them to cover up the mess we'd made in their offices.

Someone had done a thorough job of lashing the canvas into place. After breaking a fingernail unknotting the ropes, I found someone had been equally concerned that his merchandise not get accidentally wet. Underneath the heavy canvas wrappings, the mound of merchandise had been carefully sheathed in heavy layers of industrial plastic. I'd seen the same sort of sheathing in bomb dumps back in Nam.

I flipped the canvas onto the floor and with nothing more on my mind than idle curiosity, smoothed out the plastic to find out what was in the mound. Indistinctly but still legibly the words in heavy black script came through: "Via MacDill, AFB."

I felt a sudden shock of excitement surge up my spine, and with an almost audible click, a couple of the pieces fell into place in my mind. I went back to the office.

Mendoza had found the inevitable bottle of brandy and he and Halloran were calmly sipping away.

"Got that big knife of yours, Sergeant?" I asked.

"Sure thing, Major." He got to his feet and handed me the knife.

"Come on," I said. "I think I'm going to need some muscle."

He stood beside me while I smoothed out the plastic. When the name became legible, he whistled softly. With one slash of the knife he laid bare the top case.

The address was clear enough. "Colonel T. O. Jamieson, Assistant Chief, AFCD, Riggs AFB, Tullegeville, Ga." The shipper was T-5 F. O. Smith, Ubon, Thailand. I racked my mind for an F. O. Smith on the base I had just come from and came up with nothing. That's not so surprising. You get close to your own crew, but with the rotation, the short enlistments and the turnover these days, you don't get to know many of the enlisted personnel.

"Who's Smith?" Halloran asked sharply.

"Doesn't ring a bell at all. Probably a cover name." I said.

"Maybe that's what it's supposed to do—ring no bells," he said.

"What's AFCD?" I asked.

"Air Force Chaplain Division," he answered. "There's only one problem with that."

I looked at him with raised eyebrows.

"Colonel T. O. Jamieson isn't at Riggs. He caught it four months ago in a helicopter in Vietnam. Too bad—a good man."

"That doesn't mean much, Sergeant," I said. "You know how these things are. No matter how high the chaplain rates on the base, his requisitions wait till there's an open spot on a cargo plane. Could take months."

Halloran eyed me quizzically.

"What's wrong?"

"This case is coming from Ubon. It's not going. So far as I know, I never heard of chaplains shipping Bibles back from an overseas base."

His big grin took the sting out of it.

"Open it up, Sergeant." He leaned over, grabbed one end of the crate and heaved. Nothing happened.

"Better take an end, Major." Even with the two of us, it was a struggle. We set it out on the floor. Halloran slid his knife under one of the boards. The shriek of the pulling nail in the slat was oddly loud in the silence of the warehouse. He slipped his fingers under the board and gave a heave. The board gave way and he dropped it on the floor, bent over the crate and peered inside.

He straightened up and looked at me with wide eyes.

"Take a look, Major."

I squatted down and slowly reached into the box. The AK-47 is a mean-looking weapon and in Vietcong hands has done incalculable damage to men and machines. I've seen its heavy slugs open up a jeep like a sardine can, neatly slicing its occupants into two bloody halves.

Halloran took out another gun. He ran his hand along the barrel, then with swiftly moving hands, field-stripped it. He laid the pieces on the floor in careful order, examined each one in turn, holding it up to the light.

"Like it says in the catalogues, Major. 'Used and reconditioned.'"

There were eight cases of guns in all—a total of ninety-six of one of the finest automatic rifles in the world. Halloran and I were so wrapped up in our examination that we didn't hear Papa Mendoza approaching. He didn't seem surprised or especially interested.

"My, my," was all he said on seeing the cases. "What people will do to make a dollar," and he turned on his heel and returned to the office.

Halloran looked at him through narrowed eyes.

"By the way, Papa, did you call Hernandez?"

Mendoza said over his shoulder, "All in good time, Sergeant. Everything must be arranged and the poor captain needs his sleep."

"That's funny," Halloran said thoughtfully. "I never heard tell of him walking away from money before."

We opened the remaining six cases. They were a little smaller than the gun crates and the addresses were reversed. This time the supposed Colonel Jamieson was shipping educational materials to T-5 F. O. Smith, now identified as "assistant to the chaplain" at Ubon.

They contained Bibles. At least the top layer of each of the crates contained one layer of the typical GI New Testaments, both Catholic and Protestant versions. The rest of the case was equally educational. The three pamphlets they contained were about even in number. I estimated a couple of thousand of each. The first was obviously addressed to the black GIs. It was a highly sensationalized but not inaccurate account of the more lurid aspects of the civil rights struggle here in the States. It was a nice melange of flying clubs, streaming wounds and the more repulsive utterings of some of our distinguished legislators. The commercial was simple: Why fight a white man's war? I'm not an expert on either psychological warfare or the civil rights fight, but I've slogged my share of rice paddies, got my dose of heat rash and dysentery, so I could guess that it would have a solid appeal for the more disgusted and discontented of our GIs, which would give the authors a large potential audience indeed.

The second of the pamphlets was simply the reverse. Only this time the appeal was to the more rednecked of our young soldiers. Now the picture was of the American Negro getting more than his share. For illustrations, they depended on photos of the more wildly militant black groups shouting defiance at sundry forms of authority. There was a goodly sprinkling of shots of some of our more publicity-hungry lady Hollywood stars with Negroes and there was no shortage of the idiotic boasts, threats and braggings of notorious blacks.

The third of the pamphlets was obviously a bonus to the man who took the one or the other of the two pamphlets. It was rank raw pornography—the kind that comes in a plain wrapper because your friendly postman is a sensitive soul who thinks sex is something that belongs in the bedroom, preferably in your bedroom. I watched Halloran as he thumbed through the sniggery little booklet, which featured only black men and white women.

He grunted and flipped it back into the box. "It won't replace *Fanny Hill*," he said, "but this wasn't put together by an amateur. For the kind of guys this is written for, it will do the job."

The last of the smaller cases had the familiar top layer of Bibles. The rest of the case was filled with cigarettes—marijuana, of course. Halloran resealed the one pack he'd opened to take a sniff. "It's pretty good grass," he said quietly. He put the top back on the case and looked at the name of the addressee—the very busy T-5 F. O. Smith.

"What do you make of it, Major?"

"It's not very hard to figure it, Sergeant. The Air Force has been worried about what's getting smuggled out of Vietnam and the surrounding countries. Because of Anne's ring, they thought they'd found the answer. I think this stuff makes it clear they've been looking at the wrong end of the telescope. They should have been worrying about what's being smuggled in."

"This stuff is Fidelista?"

"Fidelista, Maoist, SDS, it doesn't really make a hell of a lot of difference, Sergeant. It's typical guerrilla action. Hit and run. They're simply distributing literature designed to increase disaffection among the troops, black and white. There's enough griping normally; this is the kind of thing that could increase it. They've added a special merchandising touch too."

"You better run through that one, Major," said Halloran.

"It goes like this, I think, Sergeant. You say you don't like my little pamphlet. I'll tell you what I'm going to do. I'm going to throw in absolutely free this genuine filthy pamphlet with thirty-two, count them, thirty-two poses. That still isn't enough. I'll tell you what I'm going to add. I'll give you free, absolutely free, one cigarette guaranteed to contain pure marijuana to take your mind off this imperialist war."

He grinned. "You should have been a pitch man, Major, but I don't think the marijuana is free. That's worth a lot of dough and most GIs have got a pocketful of money and nothing to spend it on. I think the marijuana just sweetens the deal for the contact. One thing gets me—why Ubon?"

I thought I had that figured out.

"There's no shortage of marijuana and even harder stuff in Saigon and the principal cities. The real problem is how to get it up to the front lines, to the men who've been on the line three months or more. Ubon is the Kennedy Airport of the theater."

"How come there's nothing strong—hashish, heroin, LSD maybe?"

"I think that would come later, Sergeant—probably would be distributed to the men returning to the States. That would be the time to hook them so the system would work two ways. Disaffect them in Nam, hook them in the States and you've got a nice little dynamite keg ready to explode in the nation."

"The AK-47s?"

"I think they're just a bonus, Sergeant. Guerrillas are the same the world over. They rarely have a dependable source of a supply of weapons. Most of the AK-47s we've captured have been in the extreme front lines. After they've been photographed to prove what we all know—that our

Russian friends have been supplying the arms—they're consigned to an arms dump, usually about seventy miles behind the forward command post. The dumps are in the hands of the Vietnamése, usually somebody in supply or procurement. That kind of Vietnamese patriot would sell his mother's milk. Maybe Sanders, Colonel Sanders, is right. Maybe the payoff is in jewels."

"Seems like the hard way to do it, Major. Seems like if it is a Fidelista operation, they could get the guns directly from the Russians without all that trouble."

"I don't think so, Sergeant. You know how the Russians operate. They give out just enough hardware to keep the trouble stirred up; then they cut the flow to a trickle. They've done it all over the world. Even Castro can't get all the oil he wants from Russia without hard cash. Hell, we've thanked God many a time for the tightfisted Russians out there in Vietnam. I'd hate to think what our casualties would be like if the Vietcong got all the newest MIGs they wanted.

"I thought they did."

"No. They get just enough to keep us edgy and on our toes—enough to remind the brass at the Pentagon that there are plenty more MIGs where those come from. But there's one thing about the AK-47s that's a man-sized worry."

"I wondered how long it would be before you came around to that," said Halloran.

We didn't have to spell it out for each other. The pamphlets and the marijuana when you took a look at it were really small potatoes. So the few guys who were bitching were multiplied. But the fact that the guns were coming in was a different kettle of fish entirely. It meant that the men behind it were cocky, pretty sure of themselves. They had worked out a well-oiled system of corruption that extended from the United States all the way back to Vietnam. It was an appalling idea; it meant that a foreign cancer had taken hold that could spread and spread, draining strength and efficiency from the total

144

military. It was a time bomb, which would grow larger by the day, ticking away its deadly rhythm till its makers decided the time had come to make a worldwide bang.

"What about Sergeant Malone on the base?" I asked.

"You mean could he be running it?" Halloran shook his head. "No, if there's a buck in it, Sergeant Scanlon's part of the deal. But he's only a petty thief. He hasn't got the ass to swing something like this. We're talking about a system that's organized halfway round the world. There's one thing you're overlooking, Major. Just because we've seen all this stuff addressed via MacDill Air Force Base doesn't mean it's the only place this stuff can be coming in and out of."

"You're right, Sergeant. That takes brass—someone high enough up, placed strategically enough, to set up and oversee the whole operation."

"You forgot one other qualification, Major."

"What's that?"

"He's got to have gone sour. Maybe this little Fidelista caper is only a propaganda job to the Cubans, or whoever the hell is running it, but it's treason for the American officer who bribed the pilots, corrupted the enlisted men and subverted the war effort."

He said the last part of the sentence, the thing about the war effort, solemnly, and I recognized the real Sergeant Halloran, the professional soldier. They bitch and they gripe; they're cynical and they're contemptuous of all brass. They drink too much and maybe a good many of them are too promiscuous. But after all the bull sessions in the clubs and the barracks and the flight lines, scratch one of them deeply enough and you see the square shining through —the clown who really does believe in God, honor, duty. It may be deeper than that, I don't know. Maybe it's part being superb at your job, part weary knowledge that your job will always be needed no matter how many sessions of the UN they have, part being away from the United States often enough and long enough to believe that it may not be the best there is but you're going to have to go a hell of a long way to find one almost as good.

Halloran was right. There had to be a very sour man at the top of the setup, but I had to argue a little for my team.

"True, Sergeant, but there's got to be a civilian or two mixed up in this too."

"You can take bets on it, Major—and it's got to be somebody who carries a lot of clout, somebody who's damn near untouchable."

He lit a cigarette and offered me the pack. I shook my head. Something he said was nagging me.

"Untouchable, how, Sergeant?"

He wrinkled his brow. "I don't know, Major. But he's got to be the kind of guy who can move around a lot and nobody pays him no mind. He can't be the criminal type. There are too many people who'd know him if he had a record—people like Hernandez, who'd be checking on him regularly, just as a matter of routine. He's got to have a real clean cover."

The hunch that had been forming for two days in my mind suddenly took on arms, legs and a face.

"Come on, Sergeant. I think I know where El Rojo is. At least, I think a phone call will clear up a lot of things."

I started at a half-lope back to the office.

Philippe had returned and was sitting quietly beside the desk. Mendoza was leaning back in the chair, his eyes closed, a brandy glass still in front of him, and a burning cigarette in his hand.

He opened his eyes when we came in.

"Your children and wife are safe, Major. Philippe tells me they are comfortable and await your return as soon as we dispose of the matter of El Rojo."

"That could be sooner than you think," I said. "If you don't mind moving from the desk, I'd like to make a phone call."

The phone book gave me the night number as well as the day number of the FBI. I asked for Logan and the mechanical voice on the other end told me Mr. Logan wasn't in at the moment. The voice didn't sound like he thought it was at all odd that somebody would be calling Logan at four thirty in the morning.

"This is Major McKendrick," I said. "It is urgent that we get hold of Mr. Logan immediately."

The hesitation was only fractional.

"Good evening, Major," the voice said. "We'd been hoping we'd hear from you this evening or the first thing in the morning. Could you give me the number you're calling from. Mr. Logan will call you right back."

"Tampa 555-2368, and it is urgent."

"About five minutes."

Logan must be a light sleeper. He called back in exactly four minutes.

"McKendrick? Logan. Anything on your wife and kids?"

I thought about telling him, but if I did I was in for a couple of hours of solid questioning.

"No," I lied, "but I've got a lead. You put on a pretty impressive performance the other night reciting my dossier from memory. Think you could do it again?"

"Sure," he said smoothly, "but let me get a glass of water and a cigarette." I heard the receiver being laid down. After a moment he came on: "Shoot."

"What have you got on Robert Kelly?"

The surprise came clearly through the wire.

"Congressman Hammond's Kelly?"

"Yes."

In the silence that followed I could hear the scratch of the match through the receiver, then the heavy exhalation of breath and smoke. Like me, his mind stoked up with nicotine, could now function.

"Okay, Major, listen close. I'll be a little off on dates, but substantially this is what we have on him. Thirty-four, male white Caucasian, born 1936, Newark, N.J., Hill School, Rutgers University, BA in political science, Navy ROTC, commissioned Lieutenant jg, attached to fleet air arm, Sixth Fleet—"

"When?" I interrupted him.

"Four years ago. He flew F-4s, a number of decorations,

I can't recall offhand which. Deactivated in 1966, opened a public-relations office in Jacksonville, went to work for Hammond in 1967."

"Married?"

"No sign of it, but reports consider him something of a swinger. I think I mentioned that before to you. We don't have anything on his personal finances, but the Hill School background would indicate upper-middle class. He doesn't seem short of money. Spends a lot of time in Mexico—Cuernavaca, I seem to remember."

"Got anything on him like he's a homo?"

Once again the surprise came through the phone.

"Kelly? Not a thing. Nasty rumors about Hammond, but nothing like that on Kelly. Why? You got something on that?"

"No," I said. Something was wriggling in my head; I tried to put a handle on it, but the idea kept slipping away.

The voice on the other end of the phone reached out impatiently. "McKendrick—are you there?"

"Yes, I was thinking." I was. A lot depended on his answer to the next question. I was pretty sure I'd get the right one.

"Where does Kelly live?"

He laughed. "So that's where you got the idea that Kelly was queer. Sorry, McKendrick, you're putting two and two together and coming out with fourteen."

"Sorry, Logan. I don't know what you're talking about."

There was a pause, then he came on again.

"I thought you knew, Major. Kelly lives in a small cottage on Hammond's estate. It's a place called Mi Hermosa—why I don't know. All stucco and Spanish tile and lots of bougainvillea and fountains. It's in the phone book, if you want the exact address."

"Thanks. I'll look it up."

"Major?" Logan's voice had a worried edge.

"Yes sir?"

"I know you're worried about your wife and kids, but

play it cool. Don't go tangling with Hammond. You've got enough on your hands now."

"Thanks for the tip, Mr. Logan. But all I'm looking for right now are answers, not trouble. It might be that Kelly has a couple.'"

I hung up. Halloran had a question on his face.

"It could be that Kelly is the man on this end," I said. "He can move anywhere he wants as the congressman's assistant. He's a former Navy pilot who worked in the Vietnam theater, so conceivably he could make the proper Air Force contacts. He makes frequent trips to Mexico, could pick up and deliver the marijuana with comparative freedom. He could have made the Fidelista contacts."

Halloran wrinkled his nose. "Maybe it all fits, but if it does I don't see a cute bastard like that bringing in marijuana."

"It's exactly what he would do," I argued. "Look, he makes a lot of trips to Mexico—plane, car, motorcycle for all I know. If he were just an ordinary citizen about all he'd get would be a routine check. But if we're right about this character, he's an old hand at bribery.

"Besides, he's got a congressman in his back pocket. That's a lot of weight with a $9,500-a-year Customs agent. If worst came to worst, Kelly could always get his contact promoted. Even if we're totally wrong, I still think there are a couple of questions I'd like to ask him. Like what was he doing outside Papa Mendoza's house tonight while I was making the deal for the ring—and who was the big guy with him."

Mendoza's eyes opened, then shuttered, and then a benign smile took over. He got up, stretched mightily, and said: "If you don't mind, Major. I'll be moving along."

That did surprise me. "You don't want to come out to Kelly's house with me—to check out my hunch that El Rojo's there?"

"I think not," he said. "You have already called the FBI. I should not be surprised if they start thinking. I have the

149

feeling they will not welcome my presence. If you are right, you can take care of Kelly adequately, with the help of the good sergeant."

"That's not the real reason," I said suspiciously.

A crestfallen look came over his face.

"I should not like you for an opponent, Major McKendrick," he said. "You have an uncomfortable knack of seeing through a man and seeing the real motive behind his words. Frankly, the real reason I am leaving is that I took the liberty of calling Captain Hernandez and telling him of our problem here. He was most suspicious. I do not think he altogether believed that I was an innocent bystander whose only reason for not giving his name was his unwillingness to be publicly involved."

He glanced at his watch.

"If I am correct, Captain Hernandez will be here within ten minutes. He would find it embarrassing if he were to find me here. Certainly he would not want a witness to any conversation he might have with you, urging you and Sergeant Halloran not to involve the Air Force in this matter. It is best if I leave now, quietly. But do not worry. You wife and children will be safe with me and I shall be interested in keeping in close touch with you."

He said the last from the doorway and I heard him making his way down the stairs.

"You know what, Major?" said Halloran. "I could be wrong, but I think that little old man just conned us both."

I had been thinking the same thing myself. Why?

Halloran quizzically looked at me. "Maybe he meant what he said to you when he first talked to you. The only good enemy is a dead enemy. He sure as hell ain't going to kill El Rojo while the FBI is looking on. My best guess is he bought himself a five-minute start on us."

"That's what he thinks," I said. "What he doesn't know is that El Rojo is a hell of lot more valuable to you and me and the Air Force right now alive than dead. He's our only real lead to the pamphlets, marijuana and guns outside."

"Right, Major, and I have the feeling we're not going to do us and the Air Force a bit of good waiting around here till Captain Hernandez arrives. Strictly speaking, sir, I'm sure you'll agree this is purely a civilian matter. I suggest we split and in a hurry."

We went down the stairs a hell of a lot faster than we had come up. But when we hit the street, we found that Papa Mendoza had more than a five-minute start on us. Both Halloran and I had overlooked a small detail. We had come to Warehouse 4 in Papa Mendoza's panel truck, and that was long gone. It was a quarter of five in the morning and taxis in the warehouse district were scarcer than a four-bit sirloin steak. We looked vainly up and down the street, then decided to hoof it to the nearest main thoroughfare, which Halloran said was only four blocks away. He heard the sirens in the distance well before I did and hauled me into a deep doorway. As the police car flew by, red roof-light flashing, I caught a glimpse of a stern-faced Captain Hernandez in the rear seat as well as those of three equally grim assistants.

"Like Lee said at Gettysburg, Major," said Halloran, "now is as good a time as any to run the hell out of here."

I didn't bother to agree with him. I was too busy pounding down the street, feeling my drying boots beginning to pinch.

# 11

When we finally got a cab, I found out that while I may be a hell of a pilot, I'd probably starve to death as an investigator. The cabdriver asked: "Where to, Mac?" and I remembered that I had forgotten to look up Hammond's address.

We stopped at a drugstore. Halloran jumped out, came back with the address and three containers of coffee, one of which went to the cabdriver.

"I don't know about you, Major," said Halloran, "but these Spanish types got a stronger stomach for brandy than I have."

His belly warmed by the coffee, the driver made excellent time to West Tampa. I asked him to pull up about fifty feet past the driveway. We'd walk back, I told Halloran.

The wrought-iron gate was one of those *fleur-de-lys* affairs. It was wide open. Halloran stepped through, quickly moved off the gravel to the quieter grass, and I followed him. In the first light of morning, it seemed to me that the gun in my hand was a little theatrical, but the careful way Halloran moved, scurrying from cover to cover among the bushes, told me he thought it was for real.

We came within fifty feet of the house. Halloran threw up a hand and I halted. We were at the point of decision. Should we take it in one dash across the open driveway to the shrubbery that masked the house, or slide around the side and come upon it cautiously?

A quiet voice behind me solved the problem.

"Hold it, McKendrick, Sergeant!"

I turned. Logan faced me; he was every bit the FBI man. Hell, he didn't even have a gun in his hand.

"What the hell do you think you're doing?" He asked it in a normal voice. Instinctively I made a gesture of shushing him. He was a single-track man. He repeated in the same voice: "What the hell do you think you're doing, McKendrick?"

Halloran tightened his lips—

"It's Kelly," I said lamely. "We think he's mixed up with a smuggling ring in and out of Vietnam. We think he's got El Rojo in there with him. We have reason to believe both of them are mixed up with the kidnaping of my wife and children."

The look of disgust got deeper on his face the longer he listened. He summed up his feelings in one word:

"Civilians!"

He shut off my protest before I got my mouth half open.

"Got a warrant, McKendrick? You better have. Apparently you're planning to break into a citizen's house, violently and armed. That alone could cost you a year's pay for unlawful search and seizure."

"But El Rojo's a known criminal," I said. "He's involved in a kidnaping, in international conspiracy."

He looked at me pityingly.

"You got anything—anything that resembles evidence, evidence that will stand up in court?"

Halloran was studying the matutinal habits of a bluejay in a pine tree. He was strictly having nothing to do with this discussion, and the way his eyes slid warningly at me indicated that I ought to bow out now while I still had a whole ass.

"I thought so," said Logan with smug satisfaction. "Tell you what we're going to do, Major. We're going to put those weapons away and we're going to walk up to the man's front door and we're going to ask very politely if by some chance he's harboring a reputed international criminal, probably an unregistered alien, known to us only as El Rojo. If he says no, we're going to ask very politely if maybe we can go into his house and look around, because this man is believed to be armed and dangerous and might inflict serious harm on the householder. Got it?"

Halloran got me off the hook. "Yassuh, Mr. Boss Man," he said. "We're sorry, Massah Boss; don't really know white man's law."

"Oh, for Christ's sake, Sergeant, knock it off," said Logan. "Let's move."

For a moment Logan was in command. For a moment, only.

Then came the authoritative crack of a heavy gun, the tinkle of breaking glass and the french doors on the front porch of the house burst open. A man sprang through the open doors, took two steps to the porch rail, threw his leg over. He turned his head towards the house as the gun sounded again, then turned away. I still remember the look of surprise on his face as he crumbled, slid rather than fell into the brightly blooming azalea bush directly beneath him.

I started forward. But Halloran had me by the leg, Logan by the arm.

"Hold it, Major," said Halloran. We watched and from the open French doors, Robert Kelly sidled, his hand full of gun. He leaped over the railing, circled the fallen man cautiously, then stood up and looked around. He had a second gun in his hand.

"He's dead," he called loudly to someone in the house.

"Drop the gun, Kelly," Logan called crisply. As if they'd rehearsed it, he and Halloran moved in on the blond young man, coming at him from different sides. I saw Kelly's hand open slowly; the big black gun slid off his fingertips and disappeared into the azalea bush.

"The other one," Logan called.

I saw Kelly look down. He seemed to be surprised to find the gun in his left hand. He flipped it onto the lawn convulsively, as if he had discovered a snake.

Halloran and Logan acted like cops the world over. Halloran circled slightly to the left of Kelly, slightly behind him. His hand hovered over the gun in his pocket.

Logan squatted down beside the dead man and without touching him he carefully looked him over.

"Who is he, Kelly?"

Kelly shrugged. "All I know is that he's called—or called himself El Rojo. I discovered only a few minutes ago that he's been staying at the house for the last forty-eight hours. I don't know how, but apparently he has some hold on Congressman Hammond."

Logan looked at him for a long minute. The struggle in his mind was reflected in the speculative look in his eyes. He'd been down this route many times before—the clammed-up semigovernmental official who was going to deny everything.

"You did shoot him, Mr. Kelly?"

"I had no choice, Mr. Logan," Kelly said. "He was threatening to kill the congressman. When those two men inside put a gun on El Rojo, he put his gun against the congressman's head, threatened to pull the trigger unless we would let him go. When he broke through the French doors, I took a shot at him. I guess I got lucky."

Logan straightened up. "Let's go inside."

Papa Mendoza and Philippe were sitting calmly in the large living room. Papa had a gun on the elegant piecrust table alongside the brightly chintzed sofa on which he was sitting. Philippe was formally at ease in a Queen Anne side chair. His gun was about twelve inches from his bare feet on a rush rug.

"Good morning, Mr. Logan." Papa's eyes were like those of an especially bright and cheery chipmunk. "It is unfortunate that we meet under these circumstances." He nodded at me and Sergeant Halloran.

"Would you tell me what happened here, Mr. Mendoza? And why the guns?"

Mendoza looked surprised. "But hasn't Mr. Kelly explained?"

"He has," said Logan shortly. "I'd like your version."

Mendoza gestured toward the French doors. "That one, El Rojo, he is dead?"

"Quite," said Logan. Mendoza brightened momentarily, then quickly put a look of gravity back on his face.

"I heard from an informant that El Rojo might be here. I had reason to suspect that he might have murdered a young employee of mine, a Mr. Hernandez. No evidence, you understand, merely the wildest of suspicions; nothing I could bring to the police. I'm afraid I then did something injudicious. I decided to come here with my friend Philippe and determine for myself if the murderer was here. He was and I discovered that I am not really equipped for police work. I should have left the matter to my friend, Captain Hernandez. For while both Philippe and I held our guns on El Rojo, he produced a gun from somewhere on his person, held it to the head of the congressman and threatened to kill him unless we let him go free. What else could we do? We put down our guns, exactly as you see

155

them now, and El Rojo attempted to leave by the French doors."

"And?"

"And," said Papa, "in an amazing display of skill and courage, Mr. Kelly snatched a gun from the desk drawer and shot him." A faint note of cynical challenge seemed to be in the last statement.

"Quite a shot, wasn't it?" asked Logan.

"Remarkable," said Mendoza.

"Where's Congressman Hammond?" asked Logan.

"Just behind you," said Mendoza.

Logan whirled and for the first time I saw the crumpled figure on a chaise longue, almost completely covered with a plaid woolen throw. All three of us moved closer. Beads of sweat covered the gaunt, bearded face. From the gaping mouth came great rasping breaths.

"What's the matter with him?" Logan snapped. Halloran was turning back an eyelid. "Narcotics, I think," he said.

"Is he a user?" Logan shot at Kelly. The blond young man's eyes shifted away. He was debating his answer.

"Oh, I think not, Mr. Logan," Papa Mendoza said quickly and smoothly. "I think it more likely that the man El Rojo injected him to keep him submissive. As you know, I live in the *barrio*. I am unfortunately familiar with the signs of the regular user. I have seen the congressman many times. I'm sure I would have detected the symptoms."

Kelly chimed right in. "No, Mr. Logan. I'm sure the congressman isn't a user. I would have known of it. After all, we live fairly intimately here."

Logan looked from one to the other. I think he knew he had been finessed. Papa Mendoza had saved his own hide, put money in the bank by covering for Kelly. Between them, Papa and Kelly had applied a lovely coat of whitewash. The worst that could happen to Hammond now was a headline story where he'd be cast in the role of the victim of a vicious gunman. It could only get him more votes.

But Logan wasn't about to roll over and play dead so easily.

"Mr. Kelly, you've said that El Rojo or whatever his name is had some hold on the congressman. How did you get that impression—was anything said?"

"Nothing specific—just an impression—the kind of thing you sense when you see two men together. I thought El Rojo acted as if this weren't the first time he'd seen the congressman. But," he finished smoothly, "shouldn't that wait till the congressman recovers consciousness?"

"Probably," said Logan, just as smoothly. "One more question, Mr. Kelly. You said you live fairly intimately with the congressman. What kind of a hold do you suppose a Cuban guerrilla like El Rojo, whose name by the way is Luis O'Brien y Guillermo, would have over a United States congressman?"

Kelly evaded his eyes, looked slightly embarrassed. Then he squared his shoulders, put on a manfully honest face. I've seen the same look on the faces of witnesses at court-martials. It's supposed to say to the judges: "There are things more important than personal loyalty." What it really means is: "Here's another one I'm dumping to the wolves."

"You have established, Mr. Logan," he asked, "that this man El Rojo was a Cuban guerrilla, a Communist?"

"We believe so," said Logan.

"Well, we all know that Communists have been successful in getting cooperation from people whose personal weaknesses they discover. That's right, isn't it, sir?"

"It has happened," Logan said drily.

It was a corny act. Kelly did everything but twist his handkerchief in anguish at having to reveal the truth.

"The fact is, sir, that Congressman Hammond has a weakness. He's a—a closet queen. It doesn't happen often. We have watched him carefully and he is under the care of a very discreet psychiatrist. But it has happened. Perhaps these people found out about it and blackmailed the congressman."

"How often has it happened, Kelly?" Logan asked coldly.

"Four times that I know of," said Kelly. "A couple of near-misses." He turned toward me. "I think Major Mc-

Kendrick has some knowledge of—shall we call it—a near-miss."

Logan looked at me and I nodded.

"Thanks heaps, Major," he said sourly.

I shrugged, kept my face emotionless. I hoped Logan was too preoccupied with Kelly to look closely at my eyes, to see the excitement that I knew was there. I knew now who the bastard was who was behind the whole mess. Cold rage snuffed out the excitement. I knew I was going to get him if it was the last thing I did. I had to get out of the room and in a hurry.

Logan made it easier.

"So far as I can see, Mr. Kelly," he said, "the shooting is a local police matter. I'm calling Captain Hernandez right now and he'll handle the necessary details. In the meanwhile, I'd like you to come down to the Bureau offices and give us a statement on the national security aspects of this situation. There may be more of El Rojo's people around and we'd like to move on it as quickly as possible."

Kelly was nettled; he tried to cover it.

"Delighted to do what I can to help, sir," he said. "By the way, Mr. Logan, that little matter concerning the congressman. You do understand that's totally confidential?"

"If I don't understand it, Mr. Kelly, I'm sure the congressman will remind me when he regains consciousness." He turned to me. "You'll wait for Captain Hernandez, Major. You, too, Sergeant. And of course, I'm sure Mr. Mendoza will not mind taking a few extra minutes to help the police?"

He took a last look at the unconscious Hammond and followed Kelly through the door.

I waited till I heard their footsteps on the wooden porch before I said to Halloran: "I've got to get out of here, Sergeant."

He looked at me impassively. "You heard what the man said, Major. I'm the only cop here. My ass is in a sling if I let you go."

"You're an Air Force cop," I said levelly. "It's Air Force business I want to leave on."

He frowned. "You mean, you got another hunch?"

"I got more than that."

"Let me know a little something, Major, and I'll think it over—about letting you leave."

"I can't, Sergeant. This is Air Force business; we keep our family problems to ourselves. There are civilians present."

That did it, made his mind up for him.

"Okay, Major. Wait ten minutes, give Logan time to get a long way from here."

The ten-minute wait was too long. We heard the police car screech to a halt in the spraying gravel and we went out on the porch. Hernandez was already squatted over the body when we came up beside him.

He had turned the body over gently, examined it, his oval Latin face showing not a sign of what he might be thinking. Now he stood up, wiping his fingers delicately on an oversized, overfine linen handkerchief.

He looked at all of us in the circle around him with equal hostility, then singled out Halloran.

"Logan told me over the phone that Kelly shot this man from inside the house. Is that right, Sergeant?"

Halloran nodded.

"You saw the man die?" Hernandez asked.

"Yes."

"Show me," he ordered.

Halloran went into the house, emerged from the French doors, threw one leg over the porch railing, turned to look over his shoulder back into the room, then tumbled realistically into the azalea bush. He scrambled up quickly, brushing off his knees.

"Is that the way it happened, Major? The way you saw it?"

"Yes."

"Shall we go inside?" He didn't wait for an answer but led the procession into the living room.

When we were seated, he said: "Gentlemen, this case would normally be a matter of simple routine. An intruder comes into the home of a prominent citizen, using force

159

or the threat of force to remain in occupation. The intruder threatens the head of the household, flees, a trusted member of the household shoots him. Agreed?"

We nodded almost in unison.

"There is a small difficulty with that outline," he said. "The man, the purported criminal, was not killed by a shot from the interior of the house. Rather, he was shot from the outside, shot in the chest, very close to the heart, in fact."

"But I saw—" began Papa Mendoza.

"You saw Kelly take a shot at a man falling," said Hernandez. "You did not see him hit that man. You also assumed a single shot. But if the man were killed by a shot in the chest—and if Logan, McKendrick or Sergeant Halloran did not shoot the intruder, we must assume the shot in the chest came from the front. It was either fired simultaneously or the sound of the second shot was missed in the excitement."

He went behind the Sheraton desk.

"Mr. Mendoza, it was here that Mr. Kelly stood when he fired, was it not?"

Mendoza nodded.

"Sergeant, will you take the position in which you saw the intruder on the railing?"

Halloran went through the French doors and straddled the porch rail.

Hernandez looked at me. "Major, more than most of us, you have had experience in difficult shooting, even if not with handguns. Would you assume Mr. Kelly's position?"

I got behind the desk and focused on Halloran.

"Would you make a half-turn, Sergeant?" Hernandez called.

The big sergeant twisted to turn his chin over his right shoulder.

Skip what they tell you, what they show you in the movies about air combat. According to Hollywood, the accepted technique is to get on the other pilot's ass and ram it up the pipe. It doesn't happen that way with high-performance aircraft equipped with modern weapons. Ninety per cent of it is deflection shooting—that's Air Force gobbledygook for the fact that you're shooting at an angle. It's better if it's an acute angle, but most of the time it's obtuse. You're banking on the fact that if you hit the big target, the fuselage, with a rocket, the whole plane will go. A hell of a lot of time it's luck, because if you're up against a good jockey, he turns into you.

From behind the pretty desk, if I were real lucky, I'd have put a shot through Halloran's right lung. But there was no real possibility of hitting Halloran, or El Rojo, in the chest.

"Can't be done, Captain," I said. "Not with a snap shot from a revolver. With a 30-30 rifle maybe, but not with a handgun."

"Then the problem, gentlemen," said Hernandez, "is who shot El Rojo?"

"More usefully, Captain," Mendoza said thoughtfully, "who wanted him dead so he wouldn't talk?"

Hernandez looked at him thoughtfully through narrowed eyes. "It is a more precise statement of the problem, Papa."

I was so sure I was right, I said: "I believe there is an answer to that question. If I can make a telephone call, I can perhaps be more certain."

He waved his hand at the instrument. I remembered the number, the same mechanical voice came on, and I asked for Logan.

"He's on the way in, Major McKendrick. May I have him call back?"

"No. Let me call back."

"And now, Major," Hernandez said curiously.

"If you will join me on the porch, Captain, I may have an answer for you."

He followed me to the porch without a word. I debated what I'd say to him, because I was faced with the difficult problem of saving face for him. I started carefully.

"You have visited a certain warehouse, Captain?"

He gave me a murderous look. "I have."

"You have discovered that Lieutenant Frank Rivera

singlehandedly broke in on four desperate criminals—"

"Five," he said.

"Five criminals," I corrected my story, "faced them, killed them and was himself killed in the gun battle."

He opened his mouth, then reconsidered.

"So it would appear, Major," he said curtly.

"I have to tell you, Captain, that it was his courage that rescued my wife and children, who are now in hiding until the whereabouts of El Rojo were established."

"Continue."

"In that warehouse," I went on, "you also found certain materials indicating that some activities were going on that are reprehensible to certain authorities in the United States Air Force?"

He took a notebook out of his pocket. "I found," he said precisely, "certain cases, containing subversive literature, pornography, a quantity of marijuana, some packaged heroin."

"Heroin?" I asked in genuine surprise.

"Some sixty envelopes," he said firmly. I was baffled.

"Was there any other—uh—merchandise?"

"Nothing," he said. "If one can overlook five dead bodies."

"What the hell happened to the guns?" I wondered, but I didn't voice that to Hernandez. I had a sneaking suspicion what had happened to them.

"Captain," I said slowly, for this was the tricky part, "you are a man of delicate sensibilities. You will appreciate that in the matter of the warehouse, it was important to me that I consider the problem of the image of the police department. There may have been a touch of rearrangement that would reflect credit on Lieutenant Rivera."

"I suspected as much, Major. We shall talk at another time of what might really have happened. But go on. I detect a proposition."

"Not a proposition, Captain, I am merely asking that you appreciate that I too have image problems—the image of the Air Force to its public. You are sensitive to the fact that we would prefer to wash our dirty linen in private."

He looked like a slim and dangerous cat, waiting for the flutter of a wing. "To the point, Major. I am a busy man."

"I suggest, Captain," I said, "that you walk carefully down the driveway, looking behind the largest pieces of shrubbery. If you find the unconscious body of Mr. Logan behind one of those bushes, I would request your permission to leave unencumbered by your police force."

"To wash some Air Force linen in private?"

"Officially, but in private."

He walked off the porch, set off down the driveway. When he returned he had a curious color. His face was red with anger, his mouth white and pinched.

"Mr. Logan too has a problem of image," he said. "Can you in the course of your laundering do something about that too, Major?"

"I can," I said. I hoped I was right. I'd gotten fond of Logan.

I asked the captain for a pencil and a piece of paper. "I should appreciate your calling that number, Captain, and informing the gentleman that I want him to be in his office in fifteen minutes. He will object as befits his rank. You will insist, as befits yours."

"He will be there, Major. Now if you will take my car and police driver, you will be in time for your appointment."

The patrolman who drove Hernandez' car had been well trained. He said not a word on the entire trip to the Air Force base. I couldn't have heard him anyway with the siren going full out. He cut the siren at the front gate of MacDill and drove me to the Administration Building.


# 12


Colonel Sanders stayed in character. He made me wait in the reception room the statutory ten minutes, then sat in starchy silence and disapproval behind his desk; I held the salute for the required thirty seconds and sat down on the barked command.

"Well, McKendrick," he asked, "what other way have you fouled up the situation since you pawned government property?"

There are only two ways to handle the brass: You kiss their ass or you shake them up. Your next promotion depends on how you guess right. This looked to me like shake-up time.

"For Christ's sake, Colonel, knock it off. I'm here to save your ass."

For a moment I thought I'd foozled the job; then the wave of rage receded from the thin cheeks and the uncertainty crept into the eyes.

"What do you mean, McKendrick?"

"I think I know the how and the why this whole business happened."

He frowned, then reached for the desk buzzer.

I put my hand on the West Point ring.

"I don't think you want this one on the record, Colonel. It's not pretty."

He frowned at me. "Maybe you're right. We can always get a signed statement later. Probably sounder that way." He opened the side drawer of the desk.

"Uh, uh," I said. "Unless you want to blister some ears all the way to the Potomac.

He snapped shut the drawer that held the tape recorder. I found out I was out of cigarettes and he was so disturbed that he shook one out for me.

"A good deal of this is hunch, Colonel. With a half-dozen phone calls, you can check me out in an hour. If I'm right, you've got a problem that's a lulu."

"Proceed," he said.

I laid it out for him, from the night I'd been attacked, through my talks with Captain Hernandez, through the slaughter in the warehouse, the incidents at Congressman Hammond's house, through the apparent freeing of Kelly when Logan had been slugged on his way to the Bureau.

"You definitely saw this fellow Kelly from the Mendoza house?" he demanded. "Saw this unidentified fellow, whom you now remember?"

"I did, sir."

"This Cuban fellow, Captain Hernandez, is convinced that the guerrilla, El Rojo, was killed by a shot from outside the house to keep him quiet?"

"Right, sir."

"Go over it again."

I went over it again. The key piece of evidence I thought was that the only one who knew of Congressman Hammond's encounter with the Indian fag was me and one other man. That was my commanding officer in Kyoto, the man who'd sent me there in the first place.

"How did he know?" snapped Sanders.

"Because at his request, I handed him a private memorandum 'for eyes only,' telling him of the incident."

"Why did you do that, Major?"

"Politicians, sir," I said. "You never know which way they'll jump."

"Very sound," he acknowledged. "What did he do with the memo?"

"He read it, sir; then he burned it and advised me to forget the whole incident."

Sanders nodded with approval. "Exactly what I'd do myself."

I sat silent. He had the football now. He paced the floor worriedly. Some of the starch had gone out of him and if he hadn't been such a thoroughgoing bastard, I would have felt sorry for him. One of our people had gone sour— a good officer, maybe a personal friend of his for all I knew. Sanders knew that if I was right, there could be a hell of a stink in the newspapers; it might even reach into Congress. That was not what was really bothering him— any more than it was bothering Sergeant Halloran and me. What was really eating his guts out was that someone he might have to eat with, drink with, fight with, trust his life with—had gone bad, irretrievably bad.

He sat down heavily. "What do you want me to do?"

"I want you to call the Kyoto Air Base and find out exactly where Pinky Prentice is right now."

He reached for the phone, but I intercepted his hand.

"Colonel, I want to know where he really is, not where his aide says he is." I'd covered for Pinky dozens of times myself, vaguely suggesting a mission, when I knew he really was hanging one on in Osaka or Hong Kong or even Shanghai.

"One more thing, Colonel, find out what day Pinky Prentice left Pnompenh. If I'm right, it will be October 19 and it will be on the base log."

What I was asking Colonel Sanders wasn't all that difficult—for him. It would be impossible for me, because I'd have to go through channels. But he could reach any base in the world in a matter of minutes. What's more, he could get the answers. What was really troubling him was that Air Force Intelligence would have to use its muscle openly, and like all the cloak and dagger types, they hate that. He knew even if I were wrong and he found out that Pinky was innocent, there'd still be a little mud clinging to Pinky's reputation. There's always someone in the Air Force who remembers that your name was "mentioned" in an investigation.

But there were a couple of burrs I had put under Colonel Sanders' saddle. He could stomach the pamphlets, the dope, the jewels, but now a congressman was mixed up in the mess. Sanders waved me out of the office.

"Go get yourself some breakfast, Major. Get back here in a half an hour." I heard him murmuring into the phone before I had closed the door.

I was ravenously hungry. I was even more ravenous to talk to Anne and the kids. I scoured every pocket of the flight suit. I didn't have even a dime for the phone call.

I needn't have worried about that. I'd upset Sanders. I hadn't made him forget elementary security procedures.

Lieutenant Kennedy looked so fresh in his uniform as he walked up to me that I could almost hear him snap, crackle

166

and pop. The cheery aide-de-camp smile he gave me didn't quite hide his dismay at my soggy flight suit.

"Colonel Sanders told me you were here, Major. How about a spot of breakfast?" He took me delicately by the point of the elbow and steered me to the officers' mess.

"Got a dime, Lieutenant?" I asked. "I've got to make an important telephone call." He gave me the dime but followed me until I shut the door of the booth firmly in his face.

I let the phone ring a dozen times or more. The house was still as empty as my heart.

Kennedy kept his curiosity to himself till I had eaten my way through the ham and eggs and was working on a sweet roll and coffee.

"From the looks of the flight suit, Major, you've had a rough night."

"It always is, Lieutenant," I said, "when you take a refresher course in survival training."

"But I thought—" he started.

"Leave it lay, Lieutenant. Just put it down to jet-jockey talk."

He got up, miffed. "I'm going to get another cup of coffee."

"While you're up, Lieutenant, you might get me a pack of cigarettes. I'm fresh out." His stiff back told me what he would have said verbally if I weren't Sanders' baby and therefore something special.

I wondered where Anne and the kids were stashed away and that brought Papa Mendoza to mind. I made myself a small bet that the AK-47s had disappeared into one of his private caches and that he had been the one who added the heroin to the boxes of pamphlets and marijuana. He knew nobody on the Tampa police force was going to get into a sweat because of a little pot. Hell, in the *barrio* it's like corn flakes. But the hard stuff, that's another matter. I guess Mendoza figured at the time if he couldn't get El Rojo one way, he'd get him another.

A young corporal approached our table.

167

"Major McKendrick, sir, Colonel Sanders would like you in his office." I nodded, and he remained at my elbow. "He said on the double, sir."

"I'm sure he did, corporal. All right, we're on our way."

Sanders was precision itself. "Colonel Prentice landed at Edwards, Saturday at 0800; refueled and landed at Randolph at 1300; boarded a MATS C-46 on Sunday, 0700, with indicated destination, Charlotte, North Carolina. There is no record of his debarking at Charlotte and we cannot be certain that it was Prentice, but the duty sergeant reports that an Air Force colonel debarked at MacDill complaining of stomach upset. No record of his reporting to the base hospital."

I felt no special lift now that my hunch was confirmed. Pinky was the Air Force colonel who had debarked at MacDill, all right. He'd used the stomach upset gimmick a dozen times when we were flying together and he wanted to see the town.

"What did he fly into Randolph?"

"An F-4."

I whistled in grudging admiration. It takes a lot of muscle or friends with muscle to pull an F-4 out of Nam right now. Despite those cheerful Thursday casualty reports, we're taking a hell of a lot heavier clobbering in the Air Force than we're telling. I know. I've written a lot of those letters home to wives and mothers.

"You still don't know Prentice is behind this mess or even that he's here," Sanders said stubbornly.

"I know, Colonel," I said. "I know now that the man I saw with Kelly that night from Papa Mendoza's window was Pinky. He's got a special walk. So did the man with Kelly that night.

"I'm also one hundred per cent convinced Hammond didn't tell Kelly about the New Delhi pansy. Hammond might tell his psychiatrist—why tell Kelly? Nothing happened. The only way Kelly could know about it was if Pinky told him—and Pinky was the only one besides me who did know."

"It's thin," said Sanders.

"So's an aileron on an F-4, but it gets you there and back. Besides," I argued, "who else was near Pnompenh in Cambodia, near the emerald I picked up, but Pinky? Look at it this way: Pinky's supposed to pick up the emerald—for what reason I don't know. He picks me up at Ubon—pretty fair cover, an old buddy, his former assistant base commander. The emerald's on his mind. What more natural than that he'd remind me of my anniversary? Hell, he expected to be in the jewelry shop long before I got up. Remember I'd just finished six months of line duty. He'd expect me to sack out for most of the following day. Pinky made only one mistake. He's not the drinker he used to be. The sauce hits him a hell of a lot quicker and harder than it used to. So he really hung one on—maybe due to anxiety about the emerald, I don't know. It figures the old Cambodian was told to turn the ring over to an Air Force officer. It certainly figures they wouldn't tell him the officer's name. I happened to be the first one in the shop, so he gave me the ring instead."

Sanders looked at me with hostility. Then he said with more than a little malice: "Then it figures also, Major, that Colonel Prentice kidnaped your wife and children for the jewel, that he shot El Rojo and slugged Logan, the FBI man."

I shook my head. I was now certain that Pinky was the operating head of the scheme, but I'd never believe he'd kidnap my wife and kids for a lousy $33,000 ring. Hell, Pinky was the godfather of our youngest, Shane.

"No, I'm sure he didn't take Anne and the kids—not for an emerald, no matter how valuable. But killing El Rojo, slugging Logan, freeing Kelly—all these he could do easily. Do you know what kind of guy Pinky is, Colonel?"

He slid the sheet across the desk to me. I'd seen them hundreds of times—the sheets that click out from the computer after the request to Bureau of Personnel in Washington. It's all there—name, rank and serial number and how you got that way. But the essential ingredient—what makes the man what he really is—they haven't been able to get on the punch cards yet.

I pushed the sheet back at him. "I don't mean that—I mean the man."

I tried to make him understand; I wasn't sure I could.

"Pinky Prentice is a flier, Colonel. He knows what symbiosis is—what it means to sit in a mess of wires and wing, hot metal and cold sweat, and feel the bird come alive under your hands, all quiver and shudder, until it races down the runway and in an incredible moment comes alive, a living and breathing thing that's part of you and you're part of it. Colonel, I swear if they told Pinky that an orange crate could fly, he'd find some way to get it off the ground. He's been in the Air Force nineteen years, flown in two wars, hundreds of missions, flown them all from the Piper Cub to the computer bitches.

"There's no man I'd rather have as a wingman if some chuckleheaded brass-bound sonofabitch decided we had to bomb the gates of Hell."

"You admire this man, McKendrick, even though you've accused him of murder, subversion and treason?"

I shook my head. "Admire him? Hell, no, Colonel. I'm trying to tell you what kind of guy he is. He's a boozer, a woman chaser, a braggart, and he cheats at bridge. But he's a flier. He doesn't believe in that wild blue yonder crap. He's learned his job; he knows his percentages, he knows when it's time to get up and get the hell out of there because the going's too tough and there'll be another day. But he's got the guts to hang in there, loose as a goose, to get the job done and screw the opposition."

"Very romantic, Major," he said. The sarcasm didn't drip. It dropped in icy little tinkles on the floor. "A regular Red Baron."

"And screw you, too, Colonel," I said. "Now let me tell you what I really think. I think Pinky has decided that whatever he's been doing, he's had it. He's sticking his tail between his legs and running for home. From his standpoint, he's in pretty good shape. He's eliminated all the

170

witnesses against him. He's killed El Rojo; he knows you can't touch Hammond and he's pulled Kelly out of the line of fire. Whether he kills Kelly or not is strictly up to Kelly. If he goes along with Pinky, he's pretty safe. Otherwise, bingo, he's bought the package."

Despite himself, Sanders looked impressed. At least I had his whole attention.

"What will Colonel Prentice do now, Major?"

I thought I had made it clear when I told him the kind of guy Pinky is, but then I realized that Sanders had spent a good many years behind a desk. He'd forgotten what strange tricks happen to a man's mind when he's free of the ground.

"What would you do, Major?" asked Sanders. "What would you do if you were Colonel Prentice?"

"Defect," I said promptly. "He's ninety minutes away from Havana. He's probably got a small bag of jewels like Anne's emerald stashed away in his hip pocket. All he needs is to provide a special bonus for Castro, and Fidel is assured a propaganda victory that's worth having—a real honest-to-God American military man."

"And his family?"

I shoved the computer sheet closer to him.

"You didn't do your homework, Colonel. Read the sheet again. Prentice lost his wife and only kid within six months of each other."

I remembered that because I'd been there when his lovely gray-haired Jane got the message from the doctor, and within three months wasted away from cancer. And the last of those months, Pinky had kept himself going on a quart and a half of booze and two hours' sleep a day. He was unable to share with Jane his special grief that their young son, Billy, flying a totally unnecessary reconnaissance mission in one of the old T-28s, had been jumped on over North Korea by three brand new MIGs and been sent splintering into the ocean. We'd buried Jane alone, because I had had to commit Pinky for three weeks to a psycho ward in a remote military hospital in Japan. Sanders' voice brought me back from that lonely, muddy cemetery.

"The bonus you mentioned, Major. Exactly what would that be?"

I looked directly at the silent Lieutenant Kennedy.

"If you'll excuse the lieutenant, sir?"

He nodded curtly and young Kennedy left the room reluctantly but quickly.

I told Sanders and he looked startled. All I can say is that mentioning it outside the magic circle buys you a one-way ticket to Leavenworth. It's a supersophisticated modification of an F-4 which is based on a cunningly miniaturized sixth-generation computer. It's about as big an advance in fighter bomber aircraft as the M-16 is over the Kentucky rifle. There are only five of them in the world and they're testing them at MacDill.

Sanders shook his head. "Couldn't be, Major," he said, "it'd be easier to get into the President's bedroom than to get close to that one."

There's an occupational disease with colonels. With some of them it happens the moment they pin the wings on their shoulders. With some it happens a little later, but it's inevitable. Their time clock stops. With some, the hands freeze at the end of World War II; with the rarer ones, it stops at the end of the Korean War. A lot of good men die because of this occupational disease, because a lot of colonels plan tactics as if we hadn't learned anything since Schweinfurt. The occupational disease has a distinctive symptom. It's a stiff upper eyebrow when confronted with a new idea.

Like I said before, there are only two ways to deal with the breed. I was too tired and too irritable to kiss ass, especially that early in the morning. So I went to the shock treatment. I remembered the $5,500 I got from Mendoza.

I leaned over Sanders' desk. "Are you a betting man, Colonel?" I asked. "I've got up to five grand says you're wrong. And if you ask real nice, I might even give you odds that Pinky's already got a lock on that new F-4."

It really wasn't much of a bet. Sanders didn't know what kind of an operator Pinky was. I did. I've seen him in action. He's got due bills with the brass of half a hundred Air Force bases all over the world. He's spread around too many broads, too much booze and laid out too much red carpet for VIPs and would-be VIPs, not to be able to ask a simple favor like the opportunity to fly a top-secret plane.

I guess Sanders wasn't a betting man. He sat in umbraged silence.

"Who's in charge of Base Operations at MacDill?" I asked. "Is it still Sam MacDevitt?"

He nodded stiffly.

"How well do you know him? Is he a friend or just one of the troops?" I personally didn't believe Sanders had any friends.

"He'll talk to me," he said.

"Fine! Get him on the horn and see if he hasn't already given Pinky permission to take a test run in the F-4. Don't make a production of it. Maybe you can indicate you'd like the same favor for a friend."

"He'll want a name," he said. "There's still the question of the Q clearance."

"Me," I said. I have the Q clearance, the highest you can get, but I've never had the necessity to use it. But it's one of those status things we all like to have. I saw the look of distaste on his face and I wasn't sure it was because he had to make an unpleasant phone call or because he had to tell someone important that I was a friend. I counted up to six before I saw his hand reach for the phone. He stopped, then waved me out the door. It was a childish attempt to reassert rank and I grinned. But I went.

Kennedy was sitting anxiously on an office chair, like he was going to worry the egg into hatching.

"Don't worry so hard, Lieutenant," I said cheerfully. "Only five minutes more and we'll both know the score."

That shows you how much I knew about stateside operations. It was closer to fifteen when through my doze I heard the sudden scrape of Kennedy's feet, the barked "Tenshun," and I snapped to my feet too. The aiguilleted colonel and the three stars on the officer's shoulders told me this was undoubtedly the commanding general of the base.

The testy words "Which one of you is McKendrick?" from a mean mouth confirmed it.

"I am, sir," I said. He glared at me. He had a well-developed case of the occupational disease of generals: they don't like foul-ups or potential foul-ups within fifty miles of their base.

"At ease," he growled, and disappeared with his aide through Colonel Sanders' door. I was glad they had already cut my orders for Randolph. From the look on the general's face, I think he had something more like icy Thule in mind.

The voices inside Sanders' office murmured for another five minutes. The aide appeared in the door, beckoned me into the office with a disapproving index finger. I stood in front of the general at the desk, made the salute as sharp as a recruiting poster and held it.

"Sit down," he graveled.

I stared straight over the gray crew cut. The black badge on his chest said: "Lt. Gen. S. V. Merritt." The waterfall of ribbons below the badge said he'd earned the title.

"Hell of a mess you've got us into, McKendrick," he said.

"Sorry, sir."

"Man taking a top-secret plane—defecting, for God's sake," he grumbled. "Must be those goddamned hippies and college professors."

"Yes sir."

He put the cigarette in his mouth, turned his head to the right. He knew the lighter would be there. It was.

"Well?" he snapped.

"I beg your pardon, sir," I said carefully.

"Well, what the hell are you going to do about it, Major? It's your baby. You brought it home with you."

A glint of satisfaction crept into Sanders' eyes. I felt a sudden chill of apprehension. They'd made their minds up.

"He can't fly at night, sir," I said. "He doesn't know the recognition signals at Havana or the Isle of Pines. We could have the military police pick him up as he moves to the flight line, take him into a jeep—"

"Negative, Major. The Air Force can't afford an investigation, public hearings, trials. Bad public relations and we've got some important appropriation hearings coming up."

"Sorry, sir. Perhaps—" I hesitated. I didn't like the suggestion I was going to make. I liked even less the curl of the lip that was appearing on Colonel Sanders' face.

"Perhaps what, Major?"

I licked my lips. I wondered if judges felt as dry-mouthed when they passed the sentence of death on a man.

"He's got to head across the Key West Defense Command. You could order a Navy fighter scramble."

"Negative, Major," he said frostily. I felt a flood of relief. He'd turned down my suggestion that the Navy fighters shoot Pinky out of the sky. Then I saw him eyeing me. He was expecting the question and I asked it.

"May I ask why, sir?"

"It's an Air Force baby, Major. I don't want to lay the job of shooting this feller down in the lap of the Navy pilots. Matter of fact, I don't think they'd take it. They won't like the publicity of an interservice accident."

He underlined the euphemism "accident." The old bitter taste returned to my mouth. With generals, it's always an accident—unless it's an incident. I stalled for time.

"Permission to smoke, sir?"

He nodded. I lit up, exhaled slowly and he waited.

"As I've indicated sufficiently, Major, it's your baby. Let me lay it out for you. Colonel Sanders believes it's sounder from the standpoint of overall service policy to let Prentice take the plane."

"Take the plane?" I echoed in astonishment. "That's top secret!"

He ignored the interruption.

"More precisely, Major, take off in the plane. The Navy will scramble. They'll be told it's a simple interservice test. They will not be told to fire unless the direst emergency occurs. They will, in short, provide a barrier to the Southeast, a herding operation. The rest is up to you."

"Me, sir?"

"Yes," he said crisply. "You will take off immediately after Colonel Prentice and take appropriate action. Unfortunately I must be getting along. I have an urgent luncheon date in town with some members of the Chamber of Commerce. Colonel Sanders will handle your questions."

He and his aide swept out, leaving me with stunned silence and a sardonic Colonel Sanders.

"Appropriate action, for Christ's sake!" I exploded.

"That's what the man said," Sanders said softly. "To make it clearer, that's what the man ordered, Major."

My brain was buzzing with questions I wanted to ask. But I could only think of the most important.

"Will the birds be armed?" I asked.

He shook his head.

"No, Major. Neither plane will be armed." Elaborately he pushed back the sleeve of his blouse, looked at his watch.

"If I might make a suggestion, Major. I think you ought to get over to BOQ and get some sleep. As I told the general, you'll probably be taking off at 16:00."

I got to my feet.

"May I say, Colonel, that you're a no-good sonofabitch in spades?"

"You may, Major," he said quietly. "It's been said many times before. Now, go get some sleep."

# 13

You have to be an Air Force general to come up with a plan so murderously simple. You have to think like an Air Force general to understand how he had arrived at what was the only possible solution. From his standpoint, I had brought him a big ugly can of worms. He really didn't give a tinker's dam who was stealing what; he'd been around long enough to know that in a twenty-billion-dollar annual business like the Air Force, someone somewhere is stealing something from rising sun to setting sun and twice as much later. But I'd caught someone stealing—that made it my problem.

He had made lieutenant general for two reasons: he'd kept his nose and record clean in a lot of sticky situations, and he found out it was safer to stick to tried and successful solutions. At his level, he saw the Atomic Energy Commission burying dangerous materials in the ocean. He saw the Army Chemical Warfare Division dumping bacteriological wastes in the ocean; he saw the most modern cities and states burying their human wastes in the ocean. Think like a general. You've got a dangerous problem. Where do you bury it? The ocean, naturally.

The solution had a nice general type of logic to it. A man wants to defect with a top-secret plane. That's not permitted. It could foul up appropriations planning that had been in the works for a year or longer. So kill him. How? Not with noisy rockets or missiles but with a quiet splashing in the ocean. "How" is the problem of the pursuing pilot. You can't waste any sympathy on him; he's the sonofabitch who brought you the problem in the first place.

As the commanding general, you've set up the percentages nicely. They're all on your side, as they ought to be. If worst comes to worst and the defector eludes the pursuing pilot, you can always call on the Navy fighters to cut him off. That could be messy, but there must be a Navy Air Force admiral who owes you a favor.

The two planes are identical, have comparable speeds, so you're not stacking the odds against the pursuing pilot. If he's got the guts, he could do the job in an instant. He can poke a wing into the other guy's canopy. He may not kill him the first time around, but the chances are pretty good. You take fifty thousand pounds of sheet metal flying 500 mph and just brush against another one of the same size going the same way, brush them as gently as you brush a virgin's nipple. That's 7.5 million foot-pounds of destructive energy just trembling for human error. The odds are pretty fair you're going to have the biggest jumble of jagged parts of metal and equally jagged parts of human being bursting through twenty thousand feet of air.

Hold it a second, General! Aren't you overlooking one thing? That poor sonofabitch in the back seat, the navigator. He's going into the ocean, too—and he doesn't even know what he's gotten into. What about him? Yes, I suppose that is something to consider. But hell, you can't win them all, can you?

That's about the way it went through my mind while I was stripping off the stinking, soggy, almost mildewed flight suit and the stiffening boots in the BOQ. I was no longer outraged or angry—just sad. Now that the shock of being appointed the general's high executioner was over, it became just another mission. I'd killed before—the other people and my own people. I knew what I had to do now. I had to take the hottest shower I could stand, crawl into the sack and let sleep knit up the raveled reflexes of a long night's work.

They do you pretty well in the Air Force when you're on a mission that's got the attention of the top brass. The grizzled sergeant with the clump of hitch stripes on the forearm of his blouse shook me gently awake.

"Two forty-five, Major," he said. He handed me the open pack of cigarettes, the mug of steaming coffee. The razor and the aerosol can of shaving cream were on the night table. I yawned my way through the coffee, then the shave. We all take the start of a mission differently. I've seen the best of them and the worst of them: we all react individually. One of the finest pilots I've ever known vomits his way to the flight line; another eats like it's the meal of the condemned man. An Air Force psychologist once described these reactions as protective mechanisms, the body taking over and with reflective actions distracting the mind from the possibility of death. With me, it's a constant yawn, while the mind revs itself up till it reaches the very pinnacle of maximum efficiency.

I thought of calling Anne and the kids, but for only a second. What could I say? They'd been through enough for the last thirteen months, and then the last four nights, without my telling them that there was an excellent chance that I might never get back.

The other—the professional side of my mind—blotted out that last thought. I wiped my face vigorously with a towel and heard myself say aloud: "Screw you, General Merritt."

I knew I had no intention of providing my body as one more step on which he was going to climb up the ladder to full general. I was going to come back, whole and complete, and thumb my nose at the whole lot of them.

"Thank you, Sergeant," I said as he placed the tray of scrambled eggs, toast and more hot coffee beside the bed. The flight suit was crisply clean, the boots polished. The sergeant had discarded the socks I had used climbing the warehouse steps, brought a fresh new pair. I hoped Colonel Sanders would find them and the new underwear on his PX bill.

"Screw Colonel Sanders," I said. I knew I had to get back my full concentration. My real problem was Colonel Pinky Prentice and how to get him into the Jesus maneuver. That's a quick way of describing the infinity of mistakes a fighter pilot can make. Mistakes like being a little hung over and not believing the instruments, mistakes like flying over the ocean and forgetting that the ocean and the sky can look alike. There are a dozen more; they all result in the one big mistake—pulling on the stick and going into a spin—a spin from which the only way to recover is to make like Jesus. Let go of the stick and the rudder, put both hands in the air and ask: "Why me, Father?" If the bird doesn't recover in two turns, assume that the Father isn't listening, and try the chute.

In the moments before I'd dropped off to sleep, I had some fantasies like trying to jimmy Pinky's plane. But I knew that was nonsense. The crew chiefs are too good; they treat their birds like a mother with a new-born baby. I've heard you can jimmy the oxygen mask, slowing the flow of the life-giving gas so the reflexes are slowed down, or

179

put a pinhole in the hose leading to the mask, but I would have to get too close to Prentice for that.

There was one way—and only one way—to provoke him into a mistake and avoid one myself. That was a hell of a lot easier to say than to do. Pinky had spent more than nineteen years in the cockpit of an airplane. Maybe his combat flying wasn't quite so recent or extensive as mine, but he'd learned his business.

Nor could I depend on his recent years of boozing to help me. The first thing even the most sodden boozer of a fighter pilot learns is to turn on the oxygen to one hundred per cent. Just the taste of the O is a psychological lift and can make you think you're back on top of the world. You know how bad you're going to feel when you get back, but for now, it is enough to start the bird, feel it come alive under you, until it's an extension of your fingers, your head and your heart.

One thing I was sure of. Pinky didn't like flying over the ocean any more than I did. If anything goes wrong that raft is just too damn small and the whole Florida air rescue gaggle consists of one old World War II flying boat. Sure, some of the older Coast Guard pilots are great; they can spot a Sunday grouper fisherman lost in Tampa Bay in a matter of minutes. But with the F-4's range and speed of 500 mph it's not much comfort to know our radar intercept extends to only sixty miles offshore. The phone alongside the bed rang as I was closing the last zipper.

"Kennedy here, Major. He's here. He scrounged a flight suit for Kelly somewhere. Captain's bars on it." That last item put an unhappy note in his voice.

"I'll be right down," I said. "Let me know as soon as you can what takeoff time he files on his flight plan."

"But the flight plan won't be accurate, Major. He won't say where he's really going."

"Of course not, Lieutenant," I said patiently. "But he damn well has got to file takeoff time or he won't clear the tower."

After a slight pause, I got: "Right, Major."

Kennedy met me at the bottom of the stairs. He handed me a duplicate of the flight plan. I skipped the fictitious route, Westover Air Force Base, with a short touchdown at Bainbridge, checked my watch against his estimated takeoff at 15:58. We had twenty minutes.

Lieutenant Kennedy had a worried look on his face.

"Something bothering you, Lieutenant?" I asked while we were walking along the long corridor to the hangar.

"Yes," he said with a touch of defiance. He was still bothered by the bit about takeoff time.

"Shoot," I said.

"How do you know Colonel Prentice is flying? Won't it make a difference if Kelly flies? He could, you know. He's checked out on F-4s, as a Navy pilot. Wouldn't he have an advantage over you, flying over the ocean?"

I stopped dead in my tracks and burst out laughing. "I didn't know you cared, Lieutenant. I appreciate it. But set your mind at ease. Prentice will be flying."

"How do you know?"

I chuckled. "Lieutenant, one thing you can make book on in the aviation business and especially in the fighter business is colonels always, repeat always, lead and in the F-4 business they want strictly a navigator in the back seat. A working pilot in the back seat is an affront to the colonel's years and years of being a fighter pilot. Like Pinky always used to say: 'If I don't need some young punk to tell me how to chase broads, then I sure don't need him to tell me how to fly.'"

"He must be a hell of a guy," he said.

"He was, Lieutenant, he was," I said sadly.

The lieutenant who stepped away from the F-4 in front of the hangar and handed me the helmet looked young enough to be still bucking for his Eagle Scout badge.

"Lieutenant Lassin, Major," he said, shaking hands.

"Nice to meet you," I said. I twisted my neck slowly from side to side, then a bit more violently. The helmet fit fine.

We walked over to the bird. The crew chief—I caught a

glimpse of his name on the lapel badge, it looked like Mc-Donough—threw me the fast salute. It's really a kind of ball-bearing elbow wave, intended to convince the commissioned help that they're as good as you and you'd better believe it.

After staring for a moment at the electronic wizard that all the testing and the secrecy was about, I buckled myself in. I hit the canopy button and the plastic dome slid down over our heads and locked into place.

I switched on the intercom.

"Clear, Lieutenant?"

"Clear, sir."

"Okay, I'm going to wind her up."

I gave the circular wave of the index finger to the crew chief, saw him duck under the wings, and he hopped out again to show me the wheel chocks and the flap strips.

I went on the intercom again: "Two things, Lieutenant."

"Yes sir."

I said it carefully, articulating every word. "I'll fly it. You take me where I want to go when I tell you."

There was a moment's hesitation. "Yes sir."

"And stay off the intercom unless we're attacked."

The pause was longer this time.

"Right, sir."

I saw the F-4 move out of the hangar farthest down the line and held my breath for his message to the tower.

"Air Force 146 to tower, Air Force 146 to tower, do you have me?" Pinky's voice had the same old vibrant confidence.

"We have you, Air Force 146. You are cleared for 15:58 on runway 31. May we have your designation and commanding officer?"

"Control, this is Air Force 146. Designation Red Raider—Colonel P. T. Prentice." He fudged the articulation of the last name and for all the tower knew, it could have been Spencer or Fentriss or Richard Milhous Nixon.

I eased our ship out after him, got clearance for the 31 runway at 15:58:30. I gave Lieutenant Lassin's name as commander, Blue Boy as designation and fell in behind Pinky. I thought I recognized the broad square shoulders, the rapid characteristic swiveling of the helmet, but common sense told me the afternoon glare of the Tampa sun made that impossible.

The next two minutes were going to be a gamble, but not all that big a one. A sportswriter I once met at a luncheon told me he could tell Ben Hogan from two fairways away, just watching the little Texan's swinging style. I felt that way about Pinky's flying. He had style, a rare combination of skills and a boldness that bordered on recklessness.

I could picture him now in the cockpit, his mouth smiling despite the oxygen mask, his eyes alight with excitement, little beads of sweat sliding down his ruddy broad forehead. If I knew him, and I was betting my life and Lieutenant Lassin's life that I did, Pinky was going to make a fast break for it. Sure, he knew there was a possibility we were on to him, but there was another possibility we weren't. So he'd go for broke. He'd barrel down the runway and long before the allowable twelve thousand feet, he'd bank sharply southeast straight through the Key West Defense Sector. If the Navy scrambled and intercepted him, he'd apologize for the oversight, back off, head for the sea and make a long sweeping circle, then resume the southeast heading.

I went on the intercom again.

"Lieutenant, watch for Navy fighters."

The answer came back crisply. "Right, sir."

The black smoke erupted from Pinky's plane and he jumped down the runway. He flew it off the ground like he always did, using as little runway as possible.

I didn't wait for the full thirty seconds; I gave it the throttle, watched the ground speed needle its way up to eighty—eighty-five—ninety.

"Lieutenant," I said, "let me know when that F-4 breaks right."

I gave it more throttle than it needed and watched the needle climb higher.

"He broke right, Major," said Lassin.

The F-4 lifted off precisely at 140 mph. The flying manuals don't recommend what I was going to do; in fact I've set down a hell of a lot of students for attempting the same thing. The F-4 can climb to 12- or 14,000 feet in thirty seconds if you keep it on a straight line. It can fall even faster if you try to bank it either way too soon. The reason why is simple. The jet isn't an airplane in the sense that the old propeller-driven jobs are winged machines that get most of their lift from a large airfoil. The jet is a metal projectile, a rocket with a tiny wing span. Get it off its primary path too soon by banking too suddenly and it falls like a spent bullet.

I kept my eyes on the altimeter. I wanted only 2,000 feet but maximum air-speed. It moved—how that goddamned bird moved—and the speed moved up and up to 475, 485 and then 500.

"Hang on, Lieutenant," I said.

"Navy fighters scrambling to the south, sir," he said quietly. That was the signal. For the next sixty seconds, Pinky was going to be busy while he talked himself out of trouble.

As gently as you take a dust speck from your eye, I moved the stick for the scudding bank to the left. In the split second before she took hold, I could feel the cold sweat sliding down my armpit. There was a slip downward on the ground speed gauge—480, 470, 460. I resisted the fatal tendency to jam on the throttle and increase the angle of the bank.

"Jesus, Major," I heard Lassin breathe into the intercom.

"The Navy fighters, Lieutenant, remember?" I forced it out of tightening lungs.

"They've turned the F-4 northwest, sir. They're bracketing him." He had trouble talking from pressure. I had almost completed the 180-degree turn—we had slipped to 1,500 feet—and the air speed had dropped to 350.

"Give me an estimate on distance from the field, Lieutenant." All I wanted was a rough visual check.

"Thirty-one point seven miles, sir," he announced.

"That's a pretty close guess, Lieutenant," I said with a slight chuckle.

"You're forgetting the Thing, sir," he said. Then I remembered the top-secret job we had aboard.

I had finished the turn and now I gave it full throttle. It moved like somebody had cut the rope on its tail. Base Operations weren't going to like what I was doing. They take a dim view of 500-mph aircraft flying a little over 1,000 feet over a billion dollars' worth of equipment and people and I was going to have to lose another 350 feet on my dive.

It turned out I compounded my crime. I had to start my climb precisely over the Administration Building. I had to get altitude and in a hurry.

The intercom crackled when we hit 14,500.

"Sir?"

"Yes, Lieutenant?"

I flipped her into a tight turn. It felt like we were pulling about four and a half Gs, and his breath hissed through the intercom. I let out a breath of relief of my own. We were where I wanted to be, headed northeast with the brilliant afternoon sun behind me.

I relaxed. "Yes, Lieutenant?"

"Sir, could I ask? What the hell are you trying to do?"

"You asked, Lieutenant. Now can you give me a heading on the F-4?"

I felt him moving behind me.

"One hundred thirty-five degrees, according to the Thing, Major." I moved the stick to correct the heading.

I thought about the next phase of our problem.

"How close a reading on distance will the Thing give us, Lieutenant?"

"If the pilot holds his arm out the side of the plane, the Thing can almost read the second hand, sir."

"Sure?"

"I'm sure, sir," he said cockily. "Been testing this for six months."

The next part was easy. I'd done what I wanted to do. I

185

was on Prentice's tail, concealed in the sun. I would have been tough for an experienced navigator to pick up. With Kelly riding the back seat, and a little out of practice, I had a special edge. They've put a lot of useful gadgets into the modern fighter, but they still haven't figured a way to put eyes in the back of the pilot's head. He's got to depend on the navigator, and hope he's got one nervous enough to keep sweeping the sky.

"I have a plane on radar at twelve miles, Major. Approximate speed, 425, heading 136."

I corrected and throttled down our speed a notch.

"At seven miles, Major. You're closing at fifty knots."

"I've got him in sight," I said. "Keep your head in that scope and keep tracking."

I shoved the stick forward and lined up on his tail. Pinky was flying a cosy 425. He couldn't know if the Navy fighters were tracking him and he was setting up the appearance of a routine mission.

"Two miles and closing fast, Major."

"Thank you, keep your eyes on the scope."

I was closely watching the helmet in the back seat. Kelly was as out of practice as I thought. It would have been so easy if I had a single missile. I was concentrating so hard I almost overshot them.

"You're going to ram, Major," said the calm voice in the back seat.

"Hang in there, Lieutenant," I muttered. I was at the touchiest part. I had to come in fifty feet over him, with my wing tip over his canopy, flying his exact speed. Foot by foot I got into position. The dreadful temptation to drop the wheels and smash through the canopy nearly took over, but I fought it back. I felt sorry for Lassin in the back seat. I was betting his life on the fact that Pinky's lifetime in the cockpit had him in the unbreakable vise of the flier's instinct. I went on the radio.

"Red Raider, this is Blue Boy. I am fifty feet above you. Red Raider, this is Blue Boy. I am fifty feet above you."

In a flash I saw Kelly's head swivel up—in the same fraction of an instant, I saw the nose of Pinky's F-4 come up even closer to us as I had expected. I made an infinitely tiny correction on the stick. Pinky's bird made the opposite correction and we settled into the position I had expected —my left wing tip six feet above and two feet behind his canopy. I breathed easier. I had been correct in my calculations. Pinky still had the flier's instinctive reaction to danger. You always pull up. You never push the stick forward. That way is earth, hard, immovable, killing.

The radio crackled "Red Raider to Blue Boy. Red Raider to Blue Boy." It was Pinky. "Jesus, boy, you do get your kicks a funny way. Now break off—repeat, break off!"

I gripped the throttle a little harder; I knew the next move.

"Blue Boy to Red Raider. Negative. Name and destination."

Pinky's voice rasped savagely in my ear. "Colonel P. T. Prentice, destination, Charlotte. Now break off, goddamn it. Break off!" I could see his angry face turned toward us.

"Negative, Colonel."

I saw his head turn away, the slight shoulder movement that indicated he was about to make a move, and I eased the throttle forward. We moved through the air like we were hitched.

"Blue Boy, this is Colonel Prentice." He was looking across the air space directly at me. "I am easing off to 410. Repeat, to 410. What the hell is this all about?"

He was watching my wing tip over his like a hawk. He didn't like it, didn't like it a bit. Like I said, nobody flying a plane likes it when the only way out of a problem is down.

"Red Raider, Major McKendrick here. Air speed 410, repeat 410. I am easing down 1,000 feet to 11,000—repeat 11,000."

I could see him shaking his head. He was liking it even less. Most of us like 10,000 feet between ourselves and the ocean, with 3,000 more for the wife and kiddies. Like I said, in a tight turn the ocean and the sky can look alike.

187

"Five degrees left, Pinky," I said. I didn't give him any choice. I started to dip the wing down dangerously close and he banked, reluctantly, but he banked with me.

"Hold the bank into 360 degrees, full circle, Pinky."

"Right, Mac, 360 degrees full circle. Now what the hell is this all about?"

"It's all over, Pinky," I said. "They know about the emerald, the pamphlets, the dope. They've tagged you for El Rojo. Who knows, maybe a couple of others."

Silence fell on the intercom, then a big laugh suddenly boomed through.

"What the hell can you do about it, Mac? Supposing I am through. I'll be sitting in a sidewalk café in Havana at six o'clock tonight, drinking Daiquiris as a Hero of the People's Cuban Republic."

"Negative, Pinky. I'm easing off to 400, repeat 400—still on the five-degree turn." He was looking at me directly now. "I wouldn't, Pinky," I warned him. "Ask Kelly how far that wing tip is from the canopy."

For a moment I thought he was going to take the gamble, ease off in an apparent effort to match my speed and then gun hell out of it. But I heard Kelly's high-pitched voice scream through the intercom. "For Christ's sake, Colonel, do what he says or he'll rip us all to bits."

The huge wing of his F-4 inched back into alignment with my own.

"How long do we keep this up, Mac?" he asked.

"Not long, Pinky. Ease down to 350—repeat, 350."

That was when he made his first try. He did what I would have done myself, put the nose down and try to outrun me on the same course. He could have done it but he forgot the ailerons were giving away every change of direction of his mind. For one frightening moment, I thought our wing tip had grazed his fuselage, and then our bird picked up the challenge of more speed.

"Altitude 6,000," the intercom said. It was the calm voice of Lieutenant Lassin and I think it shook Pinky more deeply than a scream might have.

"Thank you," Pinky said mechanically. "Easing off at 350 miles per hour at 3,000 feet. Repeat, 350 miles at 3,000 feet."

"Correction, Colonel," I said. "Easing off at 300 miles per hour at 500 feet. Repeat, 300 miles per hour at 500 feet."

He took a quick look at the wing tips only seventy-two inches apart and then came the reluctant "Roger." We eased round the huge circle, and the white-capped waves looked like the open mouth of a school of sharks ready to snap at the two planes, locked together as closely as sardines in a can.

He was calm and conversational when he came on again.

"Mac, you remember don't you that at 300, this F-4 is a dog, a dog with really sharp teeth that can turn around and bite you in the ass!"

"I remember, Pinky," I said. "Ease it off to 285."

"Jesus, Mac, you're out of your mind."

"Repeat if you will, Colonel."

"I said you're out of your mind." I heard him the first time. I wanted to be sure that the thin thread of concern was peeking through the hearty confidence. It was. He knew as well as I that we were inches off stalling speed.

"What do you think you'll do, Mac? Run us out of gas?"

"Could be," I said. He didn't know how right he was. He wasn't looking at my gauge. I'd used more fuel than he had on my run to the sun. I had to make my move soon. I thought it was almost time. He was playing cobra to my mongoose, not acting, but reacting to my move and command.

I had gas enough for four minutes and the run home. But I had to find out something. What made him do it.

"Pinky, please remain on course."

"Roger," he said. His head was turning in all directions as erratically as one of those steel balls in a bagatelle machine. He was getting desperate.

"Why did you do it, Pinky?" I asked.

"This frigging war," he said.

"It's no worse than the next one," I said. "They're all bad."

"What the hell do you know about it, Mac?" he shouted. "What the hell did it cost you?"

There was a wild edge to his voice that I'd never heard before, not on the base, not in the Officers' Club, not in the air. I was trying to find an answer when he cut me off.

"I lost Jane and I lost Billy. The poor innocent sonofabitch. They set him up for it. A lousy T-28 against three MIGs. The dirty bastards, they never gave him a chance. The no good—" The stream of obscenities shrilled higher and higher. There was a keening anguish in the high-pitched spate of vulgarity. It reminded me of the moans of a hound bitch in Georgia who had just had her pups taken from her.

"Ease it off, Pinky," I said. "It won't bring him back."

"No," he said. "It won't bring him back."

I looked at the fuel gauge. We were skating on the thinnest of edges. I could still cut and run home and take my lumps from Sanders and General Merritt.

"You were entitled, Pinky, God knows. But what about Anne and the kids? Why kidnap them?"

The intercom spat back at me. "Jesus, Mac, you of all people to ask that. I had to take them."

I still didn't believe it. "You mean a lousy emerald was worth all that to you?"

I could see him through the Plexiglas shaking his head in annoyance.

"Emeralds, who gives a damn about emeralds? Don't you understand, Mac? It wasn't the emeralds. I've only got nineteen and a half years in. I needed the other six months."

I goddamned nearly rammed him. It couldn't be as simple as that and I nearly let go my hold on the stick.

"You mean, you took Anne and the kids so I'd keep quiet?"

He'd done it so many times before, given me the earnest argument, that I knew his eyes behind the helmet were squinting up in sincerity.

"Jesus, Mac. You've got to look at it my way. I had to keep you quiet. If you found out about the emerald, you'd know I was mixed up in it. What would you have done, Mac? I'll tell you. You wouldn't have done a goddamned thing to cover up for me. You're the original square from Kalamazoo—hundred per cent straight arrow. Don't you see? Anne and the kids were the only hold I had on you. If I could keep you quiet for six months, you were hooked. You could never talk. I had to get that pension, Mac. Jesus, I've earned it, the hard way."

"They could have been killed, Pinky," I said as gently as you talk to a sick man.

"Sure, they could have been, Mac," he said, "but look at it my way. Christ, I put in twenty years, twenty long years. I lost Jane, I lost Billy. The pension was all I had left."

I suppose I should have been angry, bitter with rage, surging with the instinct to kill. I wasn't. He was a pathetic old man. Like all of us, he'd talked, dreamed, boozed over what he'd do when he retired. In the incredible maze of violence and murder and treason, the only reality to him was the storied pension. He gave me no choice.

"I'm breaking off, Pinky," I said. I banked right, the planes parted and he started to pull ahead. I counted ten, then flipped it back, jammed on full power. The outraged plane gave a violent shudder, righted itself, raced ahead and I aimed it right at his cockpit.

He responded like fighter pilots the world over. He yawed left as I overshot him; then he threw it into a violent bank right because I'd given him the dream opportunity. I'd given him the vulnerable tail to work on. I let him pull to within 100 feet and then hit the parachute button. It snapped out with the sound of fifty shot guns.

I'll give him credit. He nearly pulled it off. He flipped the F-4 left to avoid the entangling shroud, realized his mistake and tried to horse it straight up.

"He's spinning," the unemotional voice said behind me. "He's in."

I closed my eyes for just a moment, then pulled her up on a slow climb to 5,000, made the turn back over the spot. There was no sign of where they'd gone in.

191

"Shall I drop a dye marker?" asked Lieutenant Lassin. I waited a moment before I answered.

"Not unless it's blood red."

I got a jeep home from the base. I left all the questions to young Lassin. He'd seen it better than I. I pushed the doorbell on my house and there was no answer. I pushed the door open.

The kids were all in the living room. They were surrounded by a half-acre of new toys. Papa Mendoza was sitting in my favorite chair. He was beaming at them.

I went back to the kitchen. Anne was sitting at the breakfast counter on her favorite high stool. She was licking a pencil and making some notes on a piece of paper. She looked up, turned her face up for a kiss.

"Hi, dear," she said. "You're home early. That's very nice."

I rubbed the palm of my hand up and down her back. She felt warm and smelled good.

"Why is it nice I'm home early?"

She smiled delightedly. "Mr. Mendoza is taking us all out to dinner. If we leave early, we can get back in time."

"In time for what?"

"In time to meet the man," she said with a touch of impatience.

"What man?" I asked.

"Why, the man from the automobile agency," she said. "The one who's coming to talk about a new car. Isn't Mr. Mendoza right? Didn't you make $5,500 from some kind of business project with him?"

I looked at her closely. Her face was screwed up with anxiety.

"Yes, he's right, dear. I did make some money. Now give me another kiss. If we're going out early, I'll have to change my clothes."